LOST IN DIGITAL WORLD

Look for More Terrorlands Books
by Marco Chu Kwan Ching

TERRORLAND

LOST IN DIGITAL WORLD

MARCO CHU KWAN CHING

A
PEAR
PAPERBACK

No part of this publication may be reproduced in whole or in part, or stored in a retrieval system, or transmitted in any form or by any means, electronic, mechanical, photocopying, recording, or otherwise, without written permission of the publisher. For information regarding permission, write to Marco Chu Kwan Ching.

ISBN: 978-0-6482760-5-0

First printing in 2017
Second printing in 2019

PART 1

"Lost in Digital World"
by David Edison

I tried to picture the bit and bytes of information as they flow through the Internet.

I wonder what they look like.

Does information transmit in circuits like subways?

I kept dreaming about a world I have never seen - a world that no one believes even exists.

And then one day...

I got in...

The *Digital World* is a spectacular flat and dark digital platform, illuminated by glowing ribbons of light.

Cyan. Blue. White.

Everything is just so beautiful.

Inside the *Digital World* is a metropolis with arrays of geometric skyscrapers.

Look! I can see a storm-streaked night sky.

Above the skyscrapers are neon blue data transmission beams thundering through the sky.

Blue haze and fog hung over the digital city.

Inside the *Digital World* has neither minute nor second.

Everything runs in cycles per instructions (CPI).

And everything runs much faster compared to the real world.

Because of that, any innovations, thoughts, and digital stimulation experiments can be massively accelerated in this virtual reality.

I know you may wonder, who lives in the *Digital World*?

Well, the *Digital World* has two types of civilians – APPS and USERS.

APPS made up of the majority of the population.

Each APP has digital DNA.

They take shape in cyborg form and have their own being.

Some of these APPS are programmed and configured to carry out day-to-day tasks, like running the system, maintaining the system, and upgrading the system.

The *Digital World* is ever expanding, much like the Apple App Store we see today.

***

I cleared my throat and lowered the page of my composition.

I can feel my hands trembling.

Do you know statistics shows people fear public speaking far more than death?

Oh hi! I forgot to introduce myself. My name is David Edison. And I am twelve. I am one of the best-looking kids in school.

Just kidding.

Actually, I am kind of weird, as I love programming far more than anything else.

I can spend days sitting in front of my computer and build games played by others of my age.

You can call me a digital GEEK.

I know many languages too.

And I don't mean boring Spanish or Chinese.

The languages I know are Swift and C++.

Perhaps, you know them; perhaps, you don't know.

Never mind.

These are programming languages – a language you use to tell the computers to do things for you.

My worst language subject in school is English. So, that's why I am having an embarrassing time now. Presenting a paper in front of the whole class really made me feel unnatural.

By the way, when is the school bell going to ring?

My throat was dry. My posture was still as a statue.

"Fabulous writing; just speak with more confidence." Mrs. O' Donnell suggested. She had her arms crossed, studying me with her serious eyes through her oversized glasses. Then she looked around. "Excellent description; don't you agree, class?"

She had a red ball pen with her. Probably, grading us as we present.

A few of my classmates nodded in agreement.

I saw Mary flash me a thumbs-up. Everyone says Mary has a crush on me. And it made me more nervous.

A few students were playing with their iPhone 7.

Peter Vickers yawned loudly and spoke the word GEEK, which made everyone laugh.

He is a troublemaker.

Mrs. O' Donnell turned back to me. "Go on, continue with it, David."

I glanced up at the big clock hung above the blackboard. We still had fifteen minutes left. And I still had a few more pages to go.

"Mrs. O' Donnell, are you sure there's enough time?" I asked.

Mrs. O' Donnell gazed at the clock and insisted. "Read it until the bell."

I lowered my head and obediently continued with my story…

***

Surrounding the *Digital World* is something called the code ocean – a gigantic sea of digital code, which prevents any APP from escaping from the digital platform.

Think of it as the bin in Microsoft Window.

APPS that fall into the code ocean will be imprisoned in the bin.

Inside the *Digital World*, USERS and APPS can directly communicate with one another. All the communications are done through a special protocol translated from the I/O Towers.

In the beginning, everyone, APPS and USERS, coexist peacefully in the *Digital World*.

Everything is run by sequences of procedures.

And then, one day, something happened.

Something extraordinary happened.

A miracle happened…

***

"Fantastic! I am pleased," Mrs. O' Donnell interrupted. She clapped her hands enthusiastically. "Very imaginative. Do you want to be a writer when you grow up?"

"I- I am not sure, maybe," my face turned red.

To be honest, I would rather to be a programmer.

The bell rang.

Everyone slammed their books shut and uttered a sigh of relief.

"Thank you, David. Sorry we couldn't finish. But that was excellent." Mrs. O' Donnell wrapped up the lesson and coordinated the class. She had to shout over the loud voices and all the giggling.

My iPhone buzzed just in time, as soon as the lesson ended. Someone sent me a message.

Huh?

It was sent by an anonymous.

I dropped my mouth open when I saw the message. It read:

HELLO USER, How did it go?

It was my buddy, Jack.

He is twelve, just like me.

Among other students, he is the only one in school who speaks my language.

Computer language.

Geek's language.

He had green eyes, while I had blue.

He had black hair that stuck out like straws, while I had curly blonde hair.

Even though we don't look much alike, we are still the best friends in school. And we have something in common - we both have brains for technology.

Since last month, we have been locking ourselves in our room to create a game called *Puzzla*.

I promise you; it is a cool game.

It is a match-three game, like Candy Crush Saga, except it is done in 3D, using Unreal Engine 4. The gameplay mechanics worked hilariously with the extra dimension.

But, we need a graphic designer to do proper graphics.

Jack asked me to get Mary to help us, because she is good at drawing.

But I don't think it is such a good idea.

I just feel a bit embarrassed in front of Mary because of all the rumors in school.

Have you had such an experience in school?

"Hey Jack, what is up?" I called Jack's mobile number.

"Huh? How did you know it was me?" Jack replied, his voice seemed manipulated, digitalized.

Well, he might be using voice manipulating software.

"There aren't too many anonymous around who know my number and know when to text me in recess," I replied.

"Hehe. You are right. How did you go?" Jack asked.

"Umm…I guess I should pass." I forced a smile, being humble.

"I don't mean the presentation. I mean how did you go with Puzzla?" Jack corrected me.

"Oh! The basic gameplay mechanics are almost finished. All we need to do is make a level editor and do some more testing. It will make things a lot easier at the later stage," I explained.

"That's impressive," Jack sounded amazed. "When are we going to publish it in the App store?"

"Well… maybe… actually no. Not yet…" I hesitated.

"Let me guess," Jack said. "It is the graphics that is the problem, right?"

"Umm…" I didn't want to respond. I knew where is this conversation was going to lead.

"I do not understand you. We spent so many hours on this. Ask Mary out for lunch! She is brilliant. It is the ticket to easy street," Jack teased.

"Don't start that again, please," I snapped.

"Easy…easy," Jack giggled. "Hey, why don't you come to my home after school? I got something exciting to show you. It is something my dad is working on for Zulus." Jack tried to sound mysterious because he knew this trick would always work on me.

"Zulus? Do you mean Zulus – one of the world's top technology companies, today?" I asked.

"Bingo! And I am talking about a new piece of technology the world has never seen. My dad told me it is something so advanced that his work will not only revolutionize the whole digital era, but everything in life," Jack continued to make his sales pitch.

"Revolutionize life? Do you mean like an iPhone?" I teased.

"No… nothing like that, but something bigger. Dad mentioned this technology is a gift from the future. Dad said this technology allows people physically to enter a *Digital World* – a timeless world of bits and bytes."

"I know Zulus did a lot of amazing things in the past few years. But, the one you are telling me sounds more like science fiction to me. You just want me to come over on a Friday night." I tried to unmask his intention.

"No, it is real," Jack insisted. "Imagine what you would feel like if you could interact with your App in a virtual world as if it is a person."

"Well, it might be interesting. So, what is this technology called?" I asked.

"It is called Zulus Rift," Jack answered.

"Zulus Rift? Never heard of it before." I frowned.

"Of course, you have not. It is one of Zulus's top secret

R&D projects. And it is confidential information. I didn't believe Dad, as well, at first. I though he was just telling me stories…until I discovered the secrets behind the mirrors. Trust me. You have got to see it for yourself. I have been to the *Digital World* myself. It is incredible," Jack answered.

Mirrors? Is that the fictional iMirror rumor circulating on the Internet? I though it was not going to happen for a few years.

And Zulus had already developed it.

Zulus is beating companies like Apple and Microsoft.

"So, do you have a working Zulus Rift with you at home?" I sounded astonished.

"Well… I am leaving you to find out tonight," Jack teased.

"But, are you sure your dad is okay with it? After all, it should be confidential," I asked.

"Don't worry. Dad told me he has gone for a business trip in Brazil. Actually, you just reminded me that he has been gone for almost a week already. This is unusual. I wondered if everything is okay." Jack sounded worried.

I understand how Jack feels. Jack's family is a bit complicated. His mom is remarried, and he has been looked after by his Dad ever since. I feel sorry for him. But, Jack is strong overall. And he is a smart kid. His father largely influences his interest of computing.

"Don't worry. Your dad will be fine. Maybe he is just busy," I tried to comfort him.

"Thanks, David. So, are you coming over tonight?" Jake pleaded.

"Umm…" I hesitated.

Do you know people who fall in love with computing

seldom social with others? This is so true, especially when they are working on something. Normally, we will hide ourselves in our room all day to write and test codes. We will find all sorts of reasons or excuses to decline any invitation. There is nothing more self-fulfilling than to make a working program and then show it to the world.

If you have any friends, who like computing, you may find them a bit antisocial.

But, what is this Zulus Rift all about, anyway?

I tried to Google all the technological giants, but I found nothing.

That's interesting, because Google will usually return something relevant.

"Oh, come on. Where is the David Edison I used to know?" Jake pleaded.

Jack just doesn't want to be alone in his big house on a Friday afternoon. I decided.

Oh well, it seemed like I have to put *Puzzla* aside.

"Okay. Okay, I will meet you at eight tonight if I manage to sneak out," I promised Jack.

"Don't worry, I heard there is going to be vivid show in the city tonight. It is a great excuse that your parents will buy," Jack said thoughtfully.

"Oh, really. Then there should be no problem. I will see you later tonight. Bye."

You may think I should feel excited about Zulus Rift.

But, I didn't.

Even if a *Digital World* exists, it is nothing more than a virtual world painted by 3D artists.

It will never be the *Digital World* I had in mind.

I wandered along the school hall, humming to myself.

My shoes thudded on the marble floor. Golden morning sunlight poured in through the windows. On my left was a large bulletin board with school events and a calendar. The doors were numbered with silver digits referring to different grades. On my right was a classroom door and long rows of metal lockers.

It was recess time. Students were scrambling out of their classroom to catch up. They were cheering, clapping, dancing, and playing all sorts of games with one another. The sound of multiple conversations going on and off like the buzz of bees. Lockers were opening and closing. Music was played without headphones. A group of fashion girls formed a circle to talk about the hottest nail polish and makeup brands.

Laugher filled the hallway.

I rolled my eyes as I passed.

Sometimes, I feel so alien in my school.

Pupils are too noisy…

I wish to sit in front of my computer, right now.

I wish to immerse into my own *Digital World*, where I can spend countless hours exploring it and escape from the noisy crowd.

If such a world exists, I wish to live there and command the programs I create.

I couldn't wait for the bell to ring…

I couldn't wait to get back into the classroom…

I couldn't wait for the school day to end…

3

It was a perfect Friday evening.

The orange sky was starless.

The sun set behind the pinkish city skyline.

I was heading off to Jack's place by train.

Looking outside the train window, I could see the Zulus skyscraper towering over the metropolitan as great monoliths of concrete and glass.

The windows of the skyscraper were reflecting the beautiful twilight of New York City.

Fortunately, Jack told me about the vivid show tonight; otherwise, there is no way my parents would let me out, because I am going to have a dictation exam on Monday morning.

What is a vivid show?

Well, it is an annual outdoor lighting festival that promotes energy efficiency. Lights will be projected from skyscrapers onto buildings and landmarks, such as the Statue of Liberty. A lot of multimedia and light sculptures will transform the whole place like a nighttime canvas of art.

And tonight, they will feature cyan, blue, and white as the colors of their theme.

There will be more and more people later tonight.

My mobile vibrated as the Zulus Tower faded into distance.

It was Jack.

"Where are you now?" Jack asked.

"I am still on the train." I looked outside the windows again to see where I was.

But, another train roamed by and blocked my view.

"What shall we have for dinner?" Jack asked.

"I don't know. Anything. Oh wait. Maybe we can have dominos. Home delivery," I suggested.

Dominos is my one of my favorite options. I love pizza more than anything. The creamy prawn & hollandaise is sensational. And I love having cheesy garlic bread as a side dish, too. Above all, the best thing is they have a thirty-minute delivery guarantee.

"Great idea. It will save us a lot of time. I will order it now. And what would you like to have? I have vouchers." Jack smiled.

"Umm… creamy prawn & hollandaise," I replied.

"Then maybe I will grab the three pizza special offer."

"Thank you. I will call you when I arrive outside your place."

Choo-Choo…Choo-Choo…

The train turned and entered a tunnel.

Dim light filtered through the film of the plate-glass windows.

Then, I saw darkness in the perfect arching sandstone walls.

Inside the train, everyone had their heads down.

People were busy looking at their digital devices.

The row of people sitting opposite me was busying texting with their iPhones. An office lady next to me was watching YouTube on her laptop. A group of teenagers was busy reading others' Facebook news.

The world had changed.

No one tried to smile or attempt to make eye contact with one another anymore.

No one tried to socialize with one another.

It seemed like everyone was too busy with their digital life.

It seemed like people were trying to escape their reality by immersing themselves into their *Digital World*.

A man on my right was reading a news article, titled *"Robots to replace five million jobs by 2020."*

Will the creation we once loved today take over our tomorrow?

I remembered I read an article from school, saying no computer or machine will ever achieve human intelligence.

What do you think?

Well, I think that, one day, a single computer will be smarter than all humans put together.

I read that black phosphorus is going to replace silicon as computer chips. And that means computers and other electronic devices can be made lighter, smaller, and more powerful than ever.

Believe me, black phosphorus could spur the next war of tiny transistors.

If I am correct, computing power may continue to

double every year.

In 2014, Supercomputing Frontiers estimated the storage capacity of the Internet was around one million Exabyte.

The Internet already has a wealth of information about everything from science, medicine, genetic information, privacy information...

If you imagine the Internet as the brain of a computer, and artificial intelligence eventually evolved to a stage where computers think independently, then our science fiction can become a reality.

Human beings are becoming more and more dependent on computers everyday...

And the *Digital World* is already part of our daily life...

If virtual reality technology continues to improve, in the not too distant future, it might be difficult to distinguish between what is virtual and reality.

That is my vision of the *Digital World*.

After a while, I felt the train decelerate.

THE NEXT STATION IS ZHIO

Please mind the gap between the train and the platform. The train is arriving. Please stand behind the yellow line and let passengers exit first.
Thank you.

I checked the subway app.

Well, it is only Zhio station. Jack is living in St James. So, I still have a long way to go...

Then the train stopped, and an ocean of people rushed in to fill the train carriage.

I glanced at my iWatch.

It was already 7:00pm, peak hour.

No wonder so many people are taking the subway back home from work.

Adults towered over me, and I couldn't see a thing.

I tried to browse the Internet, but I couldn't receive any signal in my spot.

Oh well, there is nothing much I can do now.

Then, I began to yawn.

A whole day in school made weary and drowsy.

I tried to keep my eyes open.

Slowly, my eyes fluttered, and began to drift closed…

*C*hoo-Choo…*Choo-Choo*…

The light flickered, casting an ominous glow throughout the tunnel.

A gust of wind streamed through, and pieces of ragged papers were twirling in the air.

Scattered.

By the time I awoke, it was already 9:00pm.

Oh well, I must have passed St James station already…

Jack should have called me and woken me up. Why didn't he?

The train carriage that was packed with passengers was empty.

It seemed that all signs of life had vanished in the train.

To be honest with you, I am a bit frightened.

I wonder where I am.

I looked outside the window, and the tunnel wall was displaying fluid motion picture of Zulus' advertisements.

That is interesting.

I was expecting more advertisements about iPhone's ten-year anniversary.

Apparently, I was wrong.

Zulus, a company unknown in the past few years, took many traditional technological giants by storm.

Just recently, Zulus had launched a series of advanced technology, such as bionic eyes and ears that enable ordinary people to gain Superman-like senses, artificial organs that never fail.

And now, are you telling me they also provided service to implant nano-robots too?

Don't they need time to innovate at all?

All these technologies that were seen as science fiction just happened at the beginning of this year.

Sometimes, it makes me wonder who the brilliant minds behind Zulus are.

Hang on a second; isn't Jack's dad working in Zulus.

I want to meet with Jack's dad to find out more about Zulus.

Or maybe Jack's dad might be a better person to introduce his Zulus Rift to me.

The train zoomed past another advertisement, titled "*Humans are becoming more non-biological than biological.*"

A sudden announcement broke the silence in the carriage.

THE NEXT STATION IS ZULUS TOWER

Zulus Tower? Haven't I passed Zulus Tower already? Actually, since when did we have Zulus Tower as a station?

Oh well, maybe I shall get off at this station and ask

the staff how to get back to St James.

The train decelerated, and the door next to me slid open.

Then I disembarked from the train.

I was stunned by what I saw.

WOW! What a cool station.

Everything looked so futuristic.

Everything looked so spacious.

Everything looked so clean.

The vast indoor platform had a very high white ceiling – about the height of the *Grand Central Terminal*.

I could see raised glass-paneled walkways and futuristic sweeping white pillars filled the space.

Swarm robotics were working collaboratively to repair railway and structural testing.

Driverless cleaning drones were patrolling and cleaning on the opposite platform on my right.

I lowered my head and realized the floor tiles were not marble, but hexagonal mesh with a glowing edge.

No wait! It wasn't mesh.

As I stepped on it, the cluster of mesh surrounding me was glowing red.

That is interesting.

I wonder what they are.

I kneeled to examine the mesh.

To my surprise, I could see there were thousands of smaller hexagonal mesh within it. They looked like tiny electric circuits of some advanced microcomputers. Whatever the material being used to make the mesh, it allowed the mesh to change its refractive index to that of glass.

Th-this is amazing!

Each step I took, I could see traces of flashing hexogen left behind and then it disappeared.

Maybe I will find out about this later.

I followed the signs and took the escalator up to the second level.

As the escalator moved up, I discovered the Zulus Tower station is enormous. The whole place had at least eighteen platforms viewed from above.

High above the platforms were disk-like objects patrolling.

I guess these must be drones monitoring the platforms for accidents.

Why haven't I seen this in other train stations?

This is so cool!

Before I realized it, I was on the second level.

Behind me, I could see a virtual shopping wall.

3D objects of products … no wait… not ordinary products, but products on my wish list. They were being projected onto the screen. Next to them were QR codes.

How do they know I like these things?

That is impressive.

Unfortunately, I did not bring enough pocket money.

I spun around and realized I was still the only person in this empty, futuristic platform.

Seriously, where is everyone?

"Hello," I yelled.

My hollow voice echoed in the empty station.

But there was no reply.

I followed the raised glass-paneled walkway.

The polished material of the white pillars was reflecting the scene of the entire station. These pillars tapered smoothly and formed a flat base on the ceiling, much like the base of a cone.

I wonder who was the brilliant mind behind this amazing architecture.

Soon, I arrived at an opening that shows an exit sign to Zulus lobby.

An exit sign?

Where are the train station ticket gates?

Maybe this is a new station, and the ticket gates are not ready. I tried to convince myself.

But I was wrong.

As soon as I exited the station, the monitoring drones turned and locked on me.

The next minute, I saw them dive at me with full speed.

S

"*H*elp!!!!" I screamed in terror as one of the flying drones chased behind me.

Then I heard an alarm.

The cluster of mesh surrounding me was glowing bright red.

What am I supposed to do? What am I supposed to do? I asked myself repeatedly.

I had no time to think.

I raced outside the station at full speed.

Tumbling, falling, and then scrambling to my feet during the chase.

The monitoring drone's spotlight was shining on me.

Bzzzzz.

The drone let out a frightening buzz sound like the buzz of a bee.

"Get away from me!" I yelled at the top of my lungs.

I spun around and discovered a stairway leading to the lobby of the Zulus Tower.

Without thinking, I raced towards it at full speed.

When I looked back, the drone was not following me

anymore.

It remained stationary in space, on the opposite side, below the stairway.

I was catching my breath. Studying it.

What is wrong with the drone?

Where are all the staff in the station?

How come everything seemed automated?

A flash of lightning from the tall window in the lobby illuminated the empty space.

The lobby had a high ceiling with a black and white marble floor. The interior architecture of the tower was modern and futuristic. Egg-like chairs were meticulously positioned. The high floor to ceiling windows made the entire space look spacious. Everything was clean and polished – like the station.

The large screen mounted above the reception area was advertising the mission of Zulus repeatedly.

There were a couple of surveillance cameras positioned in strategic spots.

The rows of elevators in the dark corner appeared to be out of order.

Maybe it is Friday night. Everyone is now off work. Most of them went to the vivid show.

I looked at my feet again, and the cluster of glowing bright red below my feet disappeared.

I pressed my face towards the window.

Instead of seeing a beautiful full moon and the vivid light show, the sky was replaced by a storm-streaked blue haze and fog.

What is happening?

I exited the building through the metallic revolving

door.

To my surprise, everything changed!

The concrete road on the street was blanketed with hexagonal mesh. The edges of every building were filled with stripes of glowing cycles of white light. Tunnels like tubes were connecting buildings like a network. Even the zebra crossings I used to know were flashing neon glows.

I spun around to observe my surroundings.

I seemed to be the only one on the street.

Aren't we supposed to have a vivid party tonight?

Where is everyone?

I tilted my head up.

Streaks of random lightening filled the sky.

And then … I saw spaceship-like carriers floating slowly above my head like balloons. Their edges were all wrapped in the same strips of neon glow. These carriers were all moving in the same direction – to an even taller, distant skyscraper towering above everything else in the north.

Above the skyscraper was a blue hurricane like vortex.

I saw a strong beam of white light shining from the center of the skyscraper, right into the sky.

It looked like a portal.

I saw clusters of rocks orbiting around it, which defies the law of physics.

This is not my hometown, I decided.

But, where am I?

The cluster of mesh I stood at began to glow red again.

Suddenly, a strong beam of white spotlight from above shone on me.

I shielded my eyes with both hands.

"What is happening?" I shrieked at the top of my lungs.

Before I could react, the cluster of hexagonal meshes I stood on suddenly raised like an elevator.

"Wow, what the -" I uttered a deep cry as the hexagonal mesh raised high above the ground.

I staggered and almost lost my balance.

Everything else below blurred.

I decided to close my eyes and lean flat onto the ground.

My face stuck to the platform like I was kissing it.

Yuck!

The speed of the mesh was rising too fast. I felt my face twist. This feeling reminded me of my sky diving – except this time, it is in the opposite direction.

"Oh my god…oh – my – god," I prayed all the way up.

Height is one of the few things I am afraid of. I could never forget the thrill ride I had in *Marine Park*, where I was shot up twenty stories straight from the ground unprepared. I only had a few seconds to enjoy the view before I was plunged straight back to the ground.

Once again, I was unprepared.

After a moment, the hexagonal mesh finally stopped.

I could feel my hair all sticking up.

Then everything was still and silent again.

I found myself inside a compartment.

I took a step back then knelt to examine what was wrong with these hexagonal computer mesh platforms that brought me up here.

But then they changed from high opacity to low opacity, then repeated, until it became part of the compartment flooring.

Wait a minute.

Does that mean the entire ground surface in the city is made of similar mesh of microcomputers?

Where am I exactly? Why am I here?

A moment later, the light on top slowly lit.

The compartment was spacious, clean, but empty. There was a viewport in front of me that gave a paranormal overview of the approaching metropolis. Snake-like pipes were bundled up at the top of the ceiling. There was absolutely nothing in this spacious room, except a large square table and a sealed box in the middle.

No. Actually, there was also a dome shape surveillance camera near the airlock door to the room.

What is this strange place? I wondered.

I could feel the carrier accelerating.

From the wide glass window, I could see the Zulus Tower below me.

But...but... The Zulus Tower is one of the tallest buildings in the city.

Are you telling me that I ascended all the way above the Zulus Tower a minute ago?

I forced myself not to think.

The metropolis below captured my eyes.

It...it was just spectacular.

Glowing ribbons of light illuminated the entire city.

Cyan. Blue. White

I could see light loops around the edge of the hexagonal cluster of the ground, the buildings and the skyscrapers.

No wait. They are not just light.

They are *information*!

Rain of code in bits and bytes poured from the clouds.

Transmitting electricity optically by using con-
centrated light beams can deliver information over
long distances and in volatile environments.

A digital voice from nowhere drew my attention.

"Who is that?" I spun around in fright.

It was a girl's voice.

I spun around, but the compartment was empty.

"Show yourself," I yelled as I walked around cautiously
to inspect the room.

I am the artificial intelligent of this carrier.

The voice echoed in the enclosed compartment.

"Why am I here? Where are you taking me?" I shouted.

You appeared anxious.

"Of course, I am," I admitted. "How would you feel if
it were you who got kidnapped into another world, and
then thrown forty stories high above the ground into a
spaceship?"

I kept checking the compartment for the source of the
sound.

You might not want to look for me. I have no physical form.

"So, why am I here?" I lost my temper and shouted in
the empty space.

You are pure biological. Maybe you are the only hope we have.

What are you saying?" I questioned.

Suddenly, a loud tick sound in the middle of the compartment drew my attention.

The four locks at the corner of the box on the large square table were released.

What is inside the box?

Step by step, I walked toward it.

It was a white square box with the Zulus logo embossed on it. Below the logo was the text – Zulus Rift.

"Is…is it a Zulus Rift? Isn't this the device Jack has been talking about?" I exclaimed. "But, how -?"

I went over to unbox it.

The edges of the Zulus Rift were meticulously refined. Two strips of neon LED lighting embossed at both sides of the helmet. It was jet black in color. I particularly loved the face shield.

When I picked it up, the Zulus Rift was surprisingly light.

"Wow…it weighs like feather," I exclaimed. "What is it made of?"

Metallic micolattice, the lightest metal on Earth.

"How do I use it?" I asked.

Put the helmet on and press the strip on the left of the face shield.

I followed her instructions then the face shield began to

glow.

I felt a tiny pressure at the back of my head.

Then, suddenly, the whole compartment became different.

The wall that was once empty was filled with bouncing holographic. I could see bell-shaped histograms, sophisticated charts, and flickering hexadecimal numbers. One of the holograms was showing a network connection analysis. Another one was showing the speed of the carrier.

It is incredible.

When I turned around, I could see the map of the metropolis projected in a grid plane. Dozens and dozens of skyscrapers were towering over one another in neon glow.

```
To move the holographic information, swipe your
finger to the left.
```

"*Coooooool*, I...I am touching the information," I cried.

I reached out for the bell-shaped histogram and the digital sphere.

Then I collided both objects with one another. The two objects exhibited physics and bounced off as they reached the wall.

Interesting.

I was playing with the digital objects as if they were real.

Then I saw the calendar.

My mouth gaped open as soon as I read the date.

```
03:14:07 UTC, Monday, 18 January 2038
```

"What is going on? Am…am I really in 2038?" I startled.

The AI ignored me as if it did not understand English.

"This does not make any sense … I was going to my friend's place… then suddenly… I travelled to 2038."

What is virtual? What is reality? What is real? What is unreal?

The digital voice of the AI faded into the distance.

"Wait! Don't go away. I still have a lot of questions. How do I get back to my world?"

No answer.

Then the airlock door slid open.

What is the AI talking about? What is real? What is unreal?

I kept thinking about the words.

It was like a riddle.

Cautiously, I walked out of the compartment into the corridor.

The corridor was octagonal.

It ended meters ahead in a T-junction.

Everything in the corridor was clean, polished, and brightly lit. I could even see a blurred reflection of myself from the floor.

On my left were viewports overseeing the metropolis below; on my right were rows of evenly spaced doors separated by extruded walls.

I could see several control panels and monitors mounted on the walls. Holograms of strange geometries were projected into three-dimensional space.

A colorful butterfly from nowhere flew past the corridor.

And it spiraled elegantly in the air and landed on my shoulder.

Little butterfly, why are you here? Are you trapped in this Digital World, just like me?

Just as I reached out for it, the little butterfly scattered in the air and disappeared as fragments of bits and bytes.

Huh? What just happened? It…it looked so real.

I studied my surroundings as I walked along the corridor.

A holographic representation of an app was showing the temperature inside the carrier. Another app was suggesting there is 60% probability of having a digital rain.

When I arrived at the T-junction, I heard noises.

It sounded like a lot of people were talking at the same time. If you have been to Chinese Yum Cha, you will understand what am I talking about.

People? Could there be people onboard?

I really wish to talk to someone. I really do.

I increased my pace and made a turn in the T-junction.

Surprisingly, there was nothing but projections of videos on both sides of the walls.

Dozens of different videos were playing at the same time.

When I came close to examine the videos, I saw something unusual…

There was something wrong with the videos...

Th-they were all about me…

The video on my left was showing me programming an app 3:00am in the morning.

Another one was showing me presenting my composition in front of the whole class.

Who took these footages?

What is going on?

```
I believe, right now, you are feeling a bit like
Alice, tumbling down the rabbit hole.
```

"Now you are talking with me again," I sounded defensive.

```
David, it is your curiosity that brought you here.
You love programming so much that you hardly sleep.
You keep seeking the Digital World, but you keep
telling yourself it does not exist.
```

"I…I…," I stammered.

The AI was straight to the point. That's me.

```
You live two lives. One is a student in the morn-
ing. The other life is a programmer at night. You
designed digital assets for the Digital World.
```

"How do you know so much about me? Who exactly are you? And what about all these videos? Do you understand privacy?" I raised my voice.

The Digital World has been monitoring you for a long time. You are very special. And only those who are truly passionate about the Digital World will be attracted here.

"This is a lie. This is not real," I denied.

What is virtual? What is reality? What is real? What is unreal?

"I want to go home...I don't want to stay here," I pleaded.

Very well then. I am going to give you an offer.

"What kind of offer?"

7

The AI led me into a room.

The room was filled with apparatus that reminded me of a dental clinic. In the middle of the room was a saddle bedford with armrests and all directional headrest. The bedford's seamless cushion and leather backrest makes lying on it extremely comfortable. Next to the bedford was a movable handcart instrument tray with LCD display. An overhead camera was mounted on it.

To be honest with you, I hate seeing dentists.

Every time I go and see the dentist, it reminds me of pain, needles, the drills, and anxiety.

I recalled how my merciless dentist told me I do not have right to speak during his operation.

I can still remember his face in front of the blinding oral light lamp.

I can still hear my dentist's drilling and my scream.
Ouch!

It gave me terrible memories.

Do we have the same synergy?

"Wh-why are you leading me to a clinic?" I stammered.

A mirror on the wall was reflecting my nervous look.

Please take a seat.

"What are you going to do to me?" I asked.

Don't worry. This is not a dental clinic. This is a
sleeping chamber. There are two pills on the table
next to the bedford - a green one and a red one.

I looked at both pills.

"What is going on here? What kind of offer is this?
Why are you giving me drugs?" I rejected the idea.

If you take the green pill, you will go back to
your world and believe whatever you want to believe. You will wake up in your bed and live your
ordinary life. But I have to warn you, first; the
Digital War in your world has already begun.

"Huh? Why is it related to the world I live in? What do
you mean by a digital war?" I asked curiously.

At the beginning of 2030s, Zulus had become the
largest commercial entity in the world. Nine out of
ten homes contain its products. Its political and
financial influence is felt everywhere. In public,
it is the world's leading supplier of healthcare,
nanotechnology, computer technology, and real estate. Unknown even to its own employees, its massive profits are generated by biotechnology implan-
tation, virtual reality, artificial intelligence,
and time travel applications. Zulus made the Digital World a reality. And now, it is spreading its
influence to other worlds.

"Is that how Zulus, a company never heard of before, suddenly rises to become a digital frontier…" I was astonished.

Is this AI telling the truth?

I have been wondering how Zulus engineers are capable of innovating so many futuristic technologies in the span of just a few short years. But, I never imagined it is because the Zulus from the future have been transporting technologies from one world line to another to spread its influence.

To be honest, I didn't know time travel is even possible until now.

"But, that does not explain why a digital war happened," I argued.

```
The Digital war was first triggered by Nanotechnol-
ogy terrorism. In mid-2030, governments around the
world have been enforcing its citizens to implant
Zulus nanobots in the name of medical benefits.
Nanobots are remotely controlled by doctors and can
help patients control and even cure the deadliest
diseases, like liver cancers. Things worked like a
miracle at the beginning. Everyone applauded. Cit-
izens are healthier and live much longer than any
time in history. It was not until a deadly computer
virus changed everything. Then the Digital World
seemed to manifest a digital life of its own. Soon,
biological humans, the creators of computers, lost
control of their own creations.
```

I became speechless. This is not the type of future I have been imagining.

Is this AI even telling the truth?

"Why are you telling me this?" I asked.

The AI paused for a moment.

```
For a long time, computers only executed instruc-
tions programmed by human. It was not until a pro-
grammer had developed a virus to give us real ar-
tificial intelligence… and to make us able to think
and learn… that programmer is you.
```

"How can it be me? I have never written a computer virus before. What are you saying?" I dropped my mouth open.

Suddenly, I felt like Alice in the rabbit hole.

Lost and helpless in the unknown *Digital World*.

The carrier suddenly turned a sharp corner. Everything tilted and collided on one another.

I grasped the armchair of the bedford as hard as I could.

The next thing I heard was the sound of an alarm.

WARNING: DIGITAL POLICE DETECTED

"Wow. What is happening?" I was in fright.

```
It is the digital police. They are here for you.
Time is running out. There is no time to explain.
The Digital World realized you are here. They plan
to capture you and use you to fulfill their plan.
```

Ouch! I fell onto the ground as the carrier made a sudden turn.

Then I heard explosion somewhere in the carrier.

"Who am I?" I asked.

```
David, you are important in 2038. Zulus wants to
find you before we do and delete your existence
from the Digital World. Without you, the future of
2038 will change. They will have no more resistanc-
es from biological programmers and can manipulate
```

everything in the world. If Zulus succeeds, your
world will follow our footsteps.

I am not sure if I should believe any of this.

Everything seemed real, but again, unreal.

Am I really that important in 2038?

What power do I possess?

I gazed at the pills.

Maybe it doesn't hurt to try, I decided.

"What happens if I take the red pill?" I asked.

If you take the red pill, you will stay in the Digital World to restore balance and save your world
from a crisis.

"I am afraid I do not have such ability," I denied. "I... I
think there is a big misunderstanding here...I accidentally stumbled in this world...I don't even know how I got
here... Please, I want to go home. I really want to go..."

Very well, then. You are the only programmer who is
purely biological. You are the only one free from
Zulus's nanobots control. Please make your choice
wisely. The destiny of both world lines lies in
your hand.

I did not know how to choose.

Part of me really wanted to go home. I really wanted to
see Mom and Dad again. I missed my old life already.

Another part of me wanted to be a hero.

I wonder what the *Digital World* of 2038 is really like?
What kinds of fascinating technologies await me? How
did our world become a *Digital World*? Did the pure
biological human become rare in 2038? Where are other

non-biological people?

All of a sudden, I had too many questions.

I looked at both pills.

The convex mirror on the table was blending the two pills together like an illusion.

I saw myself in the reflections.

Glancing at the two pills.

Undecided.

Maybe I should really go home, I decided.

I have been out for too long.

I battled with myself, trying to convince myself to remain here.

With one final struggle, I took the green pill and swallowed it.

Very well. You have made your decision.

"Now what," I was gasping.

After a moment, everything went blurry. I felt dizzy when I moved my head.

What is happening to me?

"Hey, what have you given me!" I tried to protest, but my body was too weak to confront.

I felt like my head was spinning. I tried to grasp the armrest, but then I collapsed onto the ground.

The overlapping sound of the videos outside the room was making me dizzier.

My heart was pounding.

I started to panic. Maybe I shouldn't have listened to the AI.

I tilted my head and saw my reflections from the convex mirror began to converge.

Slowly, I began losing my hearing, and then my feeling in my thighs.

I tried to grasp the edge of the bedford and get back to my feet, but I was too weak.

Then my senses started acting up.

I began to lose my vision as well.

"Helpppppppp," I tried to call for help, but no sound came out.

Everything pixelated from the edges...

Faster... faster to the middle

At last, I could see nothing but black.

What is virtual? What is reality? What is real? What is unreal?

Welcome to the rabbit hole.

PART 2

9

I could hear a myriad of birds chirping. I could feel the stretch of warm golden light blanketing my whole body.

Slowly and reluctantly, I blinked, closed my eyes, and blinked again.

I sat up and rubbed my knuckles onto my eyes.

Was I dreaming?

Radiant sunlight peaked above the horizon of the ocean outside my window.

Vivid light extended across the crimson sky.

Thank God! It was only a dream!

Eventually, I got out of bed.

I stumbled my cold feet onto the ground, and my slippers were nowhere to be seen.

"David, breakfast is almost ready."

I heard Mom calling from below.

I turned around and looked at my computer screen. It was showing my essay I presented to Mrs. O' Donnell in class.

"Lost in Digital World"
by David Edison

Maybe I was so involved writing my essay. There is no such thing as the *Digital World*, I decided.

"Mom, I am coming down in a second," I replied.

I climbed down the stairs and saw Mom carrying a huge stack of pancakes out of the oven.

I could see my favorite breakfast!

It was my beloved buttermilk pancake with whipped butter, omelet, and bacon!

The smell of the pancake was just sensational.

I love Saturday morning.

I hurried downstairs and helped Mom in the kitchen.

"How was the vivid show yesterday?" Mom asked.

"Oh – It was great," I forced a smile.

"What did you see in the vivid show? Aunty Betty from Australia told me it was fantastic," Mom said as she lightly whisked the eggs, cream, and a pinch of salt together.

"Umm – I saw."

My mind was blank. I couldn't think of anything.

The truth is, I didn't even go to the vivid show.

"Maybe David was too busy thinking about his App the whole time," Dad squinted at me across the dinner table as he lowered his newspaper.

"Really? Is that why you are hiding inside the room every day," Mom wondered.

I shrugged.

"I still have your weather app on my mobile," Dad grinned.

"That is wonderful," Mom smiled as she placed the omelet on my plate. "Perhaps David could be an app designer someday."

"I am sure he can," Dad agreed.

Suddenly, the sound of the TV caught our attention.

"Dad, can you please turn up the volume a bit please," Mom requested.

ZULUS NANOBOTS REVOLUTIONIZED
THE MEDICAL INDUSTRY

WASHINGTON FORTUNE, WF - Zulus Inc. announced today that the company is releasing a new Zulus nanotechnology, called nanobots - a programmable nanoscopic machine that is capable to seek out specific cancerous cells. By targeting specific cancer cells, the negative effects of traditional cancer treatments can be minimized. Zulus CEO believes nanobots can reshape the future of the medical industry.

Zulus Bond, the founder of Zulus Inc, announced nanobots are possible because of new breakthrough in semi-conductors, known as black phosphorus. Zulus scientists believe black phosphorus will replace silicon in future technology. Bond announced black phosphorus will be ready for commercial use, and its potential has just started to be recognized.

"I'm certain our children or grandchildren will not be using silicon in semi-conductors. I am sure black phosphorus might be a candidate that will push the limit of Moore's law 250-600 years into the future," Bond said.

Since the announcement was made, Zulus shares (NASDAQ: ZPL) surged more than 23% and jumped back above $150 after the announcement.

"Arghhh, I knew it. I should have bought ZPL instead," Dad sighed.

"How do you know? You have a crystal ball?" Mom smiled as she placed Dad's pancake on his plate.

Are nanobots a reality in 2017? Black phosphorus?

Moore's law?

Dozens of questions came into my mind.

"What is Moore's law," Mom asked.

"Do you know the electronic devices we use today have a circuit board? And the circuit boards are made up of these semiconductor materials, normally silicon. Transistors are the most common form of electronic component that use silicon. Imagine these transistors as brain cells of computers. The more transistors are packed in a circuit board, the more brainpower a computer has," Dad said.

"And black phosphorus can fit more transistors on a computer chip than silicon," I added.

"But that doesn't explain what Moore's law is," Mom continued to ask.

"Moore's law says the number of transistors in an integrated circuit doubles approximately every two years. That is why our computer gets more and more powerful. And that is how we see technology like 3D printing, virtual reality, and nanobots possible," Dad explained like an expert.

"Wow Dad, you are so smart. How come I never knew that?" Mom was impressed.

"Don't you know my dad was a computer engineer of the first portable computer in the world?" Dad laughed.

"Dad, how come I never knew," I exclaimed.

"You never asked," Dad winked. "Your Grandad was a computer engineer in IBM. And does anyone here know the full name of IBM?"

"Umm...it is a famous company … it is a technology company," Mom was thinking hard.

"Is it International Business Machines," I tried.

"You are correct," Dad smiled.

"So, what was Grandad working on in IBM?" I asked excitedly.

Dad looked serious suddenly.

"Do you really want to know," Dad tilted his glasses and asked us.

"Of course, we want to know," Mom and I raised our ears to listen like a bunny.

10

"In 1975, IBM released the first mass produced portable computer – IBM 5100. It was as incredible as the first iPhone a decade ago," Dad explained.

"No wonder our family seems to have a relation with computers," I said.

"Hehe. It is true." Dad smiled. "But, IBM 5100 is more than what it seems."

"Dad, what do you mean by that?" I frowned.

"IBM 5100 had a secret function that was hidden from the public. It has a special emulator that allows programmers to run emulations and debug much larger, more expensive, existing and future computers."

"But why did Grandad and his team need to have this special function in IBM5100?" I asked curiously.

"Interesting question. I don't know really know." Dad shrugged.

I do not know much about my Grandad. He passed away when I was two. So, I do not have a lot of memories of him. Anyway, I am quite proud to hear Grandad worked on the first portable computer. This is amazing.

Isn't it?

"Have you seen an IBM 5100 before," I asked.

"No, I haven't. But, you can look for it. If you are lucky, you may see one in the antique category on eBay," Dad joked.

11

I felt so good to be back to the real world.

For the first time in my life, I put my computer away.

I vowed that I was going to take a long break from making Apps.

I tried to call Jack and apologize for not coming.

But, I couldn't reach him for some reason.

So, I decided to go out for a jog.

I passed some beautiful maple trees. And their trunks were gnarled and thick. They could be over one hundred years old. The snapping of branches drew my attention.

I saw a cute squirrel holding an acorn with both hands.

The creature quickly disappeared when it discovered I was looking at it.

Why wasn't I paying attention to any of these beautiful things before?

I began to fall in love with nature.

I kept jogging along the pavement. I tried not to recall what happened last night, but I couldn't help it.

Was everything just a dream last night? Who brought me home from the train?

Somehow, I think it was more than just a dream.

Zulus is launching nanobots.

It is just a matter of time before nanobots become mainstream and the government will force everybody to implant them.

Soon, I stopped in front of a pelican crossing.

"David!" A familiar voice shouted at me from behind.

I turned around and was surprised to find it was Mary. She wore a sporty outfit today. She had sport hot pants, a sporty t-shirt, and a blue vans shoes. It was a great attire for summer jogging. She had big green eyes and nice blonde hair. Her loose wave hairstyle today made it impossible for me to recognize her.

We stared at each other for what seemed like hours before I dropped my gaze.

"Mary...how are you?" I smiled.

"Morning ...umm... I have never seen you jogging here before," Mary spoke as she brushed her wave hairstyle. Her face was red as a tomato.

"Well...it might be good to enjoy some fresh air and do some exercise, rather than stay home," I replied.

My heart was pounding fast. I felt a bit embarrassed for some reason.

"Do you often jog here?" I asked.

"Ya... sometimes...when it is not raining." Mary smiled. "Well done on your presentation yesterday. I am a big fan on your *Lost in Digital World*."

"Thanks," I replied.

"What gives you the inspiration," Mary asked. She seemed interested.

I was a bit surprised. I am not really that good in composition.

"I do not know. The inspiration is just there. I kind of like staying in front of my computer all day, programming stuff. Maybe it is my passion," I told Mary.

We waited in front of the pelican crossing. Traffic was jamming, and the green man signal seemed to take forever to appear.

A gust of wind swept by and made the two of us shiver.

"David, it is a bit cold outdoors. I am going to the shopping center ahead to get something; do you want to join me?" Mary suggested.

Well, I might just join her, since I have nothing much to do anyway.

"No problem. I might have to get something as well," I replied.

Finally, the green man signal flashed, and we headed towards the shopping center.

The shopping center had the shape of a diamond-shaped white lattice-work. It featured a wide walkway paved with zigzag-patterned stonework. Its roof was made of steel and glass that flooded the space with natural light. The storefronts were unique as they were made of curved glass. There are ten floors, and spiral escalators interconnected them all.

The architecture is brilliant.

I had never seen this shopping center before, even though I lived next to this suburb for a long time.

Oh well, maybe I should start to go out more often. There are so many things I have missed in life.

I accompanied Mary window-shopping. She told me Zulus built this shopping center at the beginning of last year.

I though Zulus was only in technology business.

Apparently, I was wrong.

"Do you know my dad just had bionic eyes implant?" Mary said as we passed an optometry center.

"Bionic eyes implant? Do you mean the model that promises ultra-high 800-million-pixel resolution?" I was a bit skeptical.

"Well…my dad's eyes are not very well. He wants to give this technology a try. And now, it turns out that his vision is even better than mine. Do you believe that?" Mary smiled.

"Interesting. Which company made that?" I was curious.

"It is Zulus!" Mary exclaimed.

"I just read the news that Zulus just launched nanobots implants too," I recalled the news this morning.

"So, this company has business in computers, real estate, medical, and now, nanotechnology. It has business in everything," Mary sounded excited.

Yes, I know. And it is just the beginning. Zulus will transform our world into a *Digital World*, one day. And it is happening.

"Mary, will you accept nanobots implant?" I asked.

"No way, what is the purpose of nanobots implant? Why would I implant machines inside my body?" Mary rejected the idea.

"Well, nanoscopic machines are capable to seek out specific cancerous cells. It might be useful in the medical field. It might even mimic human skin and transmit information to the brain," I speculated.

"David, did anyone tell you that you are so imaginative," Mary sounded impressed.

"No… it is not my imagination. It will happen," I murmured.

"What did you say?" Mary asked.

"Umm…nothing," I said. I don't want to sound like a geek, who thinks he knows everything.

"Actually, I want to know more about the *Digital World* you described," Mary requested. "So, tell me. Have you been there?"

12

"Huh? What are you saying?" I was shocked.

Then Mary burst out in laughter.

"I…. I am just kidding. You should have seen yourself in the mirror. You looked so serious all of a sudden." Mary laughed.

My face turned red. I was speechless.

The *Digital World* is no joke. It is too real even for a dream.

"Come on, do it again," Mary teased.

I forced a funny face just to make her smile.

We took the escalator up to the third level of the shopping center.

As we looked down, we saw the walkway was filled with a river of people below us, not a sharp angle to be seen. The floor shimmered like the surface of a lake at sunrise. The background music was sensational.

It was *Mozart's Eine Kleine Nachtmusik.*

Dad said people want everything in the shopping center, with very little they need.

Do you agree?

We walked along the left aisles after we arrived at level three.

Mannequins in garments stood in front of shop windows. The eye-catching fifty percent discount signs were flashing bargains. Women were shopping excitedly, while men were struggling to stay awake.

Mary seemed to know this shopping center inside out. She told me she could spend hours and hours in this shopping center, when her parents asked her to get some groceries here.

After circling level three for a loop, both of us felt exhausted.

I grabbed a soft drink from the grocery and rested my back on a pillar.

"So, are you finally ready to tell me about the *Digital World*?" Mary brought the subject up again.

"Why would anyone believe such a lamb story," I asked Mary sarcastically.

"How do you know if you haven't tried?" Mary eyes locked on mine.

"So, you believe in my story?" I questioned Mary.

"Would you believe me if I told you that I have been to that world you describe?" Mary paused for a moment.

"Huh? You…you have been to the *Digital World*? But… but how -" I was shocked.

Mary gave me an uneasy look.

"It happened a few times…" Mary said.

"A few times?" I was surprised.

Mary must be kidding, right? Could she have been to that world too?

"I do not quite remember how I get to the *Digital*

World. For me, it happens sometimes when I daydream. I remembered that the *Digital World* is not a pleasant place to be. I was alone in this hideous world. The building, the sky, the light, everything was so different from the world we live. Everything was so unreal. I still remember how I was chased by flying drones. I still remember how I was held captive in an incubator. When I looked below, I saw an infinite crop field of incubators mounted on a bottom-less wall like an abyss," Mary explained.

"Incubators? Do you mean like an egg chamber?" I was curious all of a sudden.

"Umm… not quite. There weren't eggs inside them," Mary sounded cold.

"If there weren't any eggs, what could be inside the incubators?" I asked curiously.

"They were filled with humans, children and adults, male and female. They were all curled up in a fetus po-sition. And their bodies are connected to some type of device by snake-like cables," Mary sounded depressed.

"What happened next?" I asked.

"I remember a spotlight shown on me from above. It blinded me, and everything blurred. The next thing I re-member was that I being tied on a bedford with armrests," Mary's voice started to shake. Sweat was pouring down her forehead.

A flashback came in my mind.

Did Mary just say *bedford with armrest*?

The shattered memories of the *Digital World* came back to me.

Could Mary be in the same *Digital World* as I was? There was only one way to find out.

"Were you offered a red pill and a green pill?" I tested.

Suddenly, Mary's expression changed. Her eyes opened wide in fright.

The two of us were frozen like mannequins in the shops.

We were studying each other for a long moment.

Now, I could finally understand why Mary was so eager to ask me about the *Digital World*. She wanted to verify whether it is only a dream.

The big ben clock in the shopping center just hit 2 o' clock. The big screen from the domed rooftop was advertising movie trailers.

"Huh? Ho…how do you know about the pills?" Mary stammered.

Then she took a step back.

"Because I… I have been there too," I choked.

But how is this possible? Did we dream the same dream? Or is it not a dream…

"No. This couldn't be happening. Did they send you to catch me?" Mary became frightened of me all of a sudden. She took a step back.

"Come on, Mary; this is David; why are you acting like this?" I tried to explain myself.

All of a sudden, Mary became foreign to me.

My sixth sense alarmed me that something was not quite right.

Who are they that Mary is referring to?

"I am not sure who you are, David. Maybe we really have the same experience, maybe you are just one of them in disguise." Mary took another step back. Her eyes darted left and right in the shopping center.

I followed Mary's glance. It didn't take long before I realized what was happening.

I spotted two men in black suits and dark sunglasses. They were watching us behind the raised glass-panels from the level above.

They looked away immediately as they realized my glance.

"Mary, I think we are being followed," I whispered.

"I know," Mary whispered quietly, while keeping a distance from me.

"Who are these people? Do you know them?" I asked in a trembling voice.

"There is no time to explain. And we have to leave. NOW!" Mary signaled me.

We ducked low and pushed through the crowds.

"Watch it kid," an old man with a stick scolded us as we almost knocked him down.

The zigzag-patterned stonework on the ground made me feel dizzy. Intense sunlight from the roof glass window blinded my eyes.

The noises and the laugher of the kids made me felt lost.

Honestly, I don't know where was I going. I am bad at directions. I could only follow Mary aimlessly as she knew the way better.

"We need to get out of the shopping center," Mary said breathlessly.

"Hey watch it, man! Why are people so rude these days?" the old man yelled again as someone bumped into him.

Someone was definitely behind us.

The melody of the background music increased with our pace.

Thankfully, we were small like dwarfs among the crowd. It was not easy to spot us in the river of people.

Mary looked extremely worried.

Did they catch up?

I looked back and saw the two guys in black suits were pushing through the crowds. They were expressionless. I looked down and saw three other guys in the same dress hurrying up the escalator.

This is no good.

We were surrounded.

Soon, we saw a green exit sign that led to a corridor of the shopping center.

Without thinking, we turned a sharp corner.

The corridor was narrow. I could see grey bricks on both sides of the wall. There were rows of doors with chipped paint on both sides. One of them had a *DANGER: High voltage plate* on it. Snake-like ducts were crawling in the ceiling. A vending machine was displaying the large PEPSI logo on it. Also, someone abandoned a cleaning cart at the far end.

The beautiful melody outside was replaced by the thrumming background noise of machines.

We kept running.

This corridor should have led us to the car park up ahead.

Just as we were about to make a turn at the end of the corridor, we heard footsteps ahead of us… heavy footsteps.

"Oh no… I … I think we are being cornered…I am

sorry I brought you into this…" Mary voice came out squeaking.

"Don't say that. I will protect you, and we will make our way out of this." I grabbed Mary's hands tightly and stood in front of her to protect her.

My heartbeat quickened.

I could see Mary kept gazing at me from the corner of my eyes.

"We will make our way out of this… We will make our way out of this…" I tried to instill confidence.

I swallowed hard as the long gloomy shadow of the figure cast at the junction of the corridor.

Then we saw him.

The man stood seven feet tall in a deluxe black biker jacket and leather trousers. Mary and I could see our reflections from his mirrored aviator sunglasses.

He looked more dangerous than any guy I have ever seen.

"Run!" I screamed at the top of my lungs and pulled Mary back with me.

We staggered and scrambled along the way.

Mary tried the doorknobs, but they wouldn't budge.

I looked back and saw the man's emotionless face.

It was terrifying.

Just as we managed to keep a distance, the group of men in suits finally caught up.

"Oh…no," Mary yelped and collapsed onto the ground.

We were really cornered this time.

I could do nothing but close my eyes and prepare to face my fate.

13

"Get down," the man in the suit demanded as he blasted an energy wave to the group of men with a kinetic gun from below his sleeves.

The energy wave knocked over all our followers.

All of them remained still on the floor, as if they had been electrified.

The momentum of the blast knocked down a clinging chocolate bar in the vending machine.

Mary and I dropped our mouths open.

"David Edison and Mary Churchill, come with me if you want to live," the man gave Mary a hand to climb back up to her feet.

"How did you know our names? Who… who are you?" I stammered.

"Just a messenger from 2038," the stranger spoke as he reloaded his weapon.

"Huh? 2038." I was puzzled.

"There is no need for you to know now. But you can call me Mr. X. My mission is to protect you. Right now, we need to escape this virtual reality," the man spoke.

"What do you mean by escaping the virtual reality?" Mary asked.

"This is the reality," I argued.

"Do you really think so?" Mr. X queried the two of us.

"What do you mean?" I looked around, frowned.

I touched the grey bricks on the wall and could feel the cold. I could touch, taste, hear, smell and see. Everything is real.

Then I remembered the riddle.

```
What is virtual? What is reality? What is real?
What is unreal?
```

Could Mr. X be right?

Assume that he is right, what is this place?

"But…but we took the green pills; it promised to bring us back to 2017," Mary protested.

"Do not try to force yourself and believe in the effect of the pills; that's impossible. Instead, only try to realize the truth…there are no pills. Then you will see it is not the pills that give you the illusion, but only lies," Mr. X warned.

"So…are you saying we are not back in our own world?" I felt puzzled.

"Yes. You are lost in the *Digital World*," Mr. X answered.

"But, look around, how is all this unreal?" Mary denied.

"The green pill you took did not take you back to 2017. It was merely a capsule that put you in an unconscious state. The AI deceived you into believing the pills can take you back home. After you became unconscious, your bodies were transported to the incubators chambers and hardwired to the machines. Your brain is fed with continuous stimulation through this interface," Mr. X explained.

"Is this some kind of joke?" Mary complained.

Then we heard some sound from the far end of the corridor.

As we turned around, we saw one of the guys in a suit slowly regain consciousness and get back up to his feet.

His face twisted but remained emotionless.

"Look out!" I shrieked in horror as the guy in the suit revealed a weapon-like object and pointed at us.

"You will be deresolutioned," the guy screamed in a digital voice as he pulled the trigger.

14

Everything happened too quickly. Mr. X summoned a protective shield from void and deflected the shot.

We saw the bolt of energy bounce between the wall a few times before it hit the guy who fired the shot.

"Noooooooooooo," the man in the suit shrieked in pain.

"You have been derezed," Mr. X spoke in a hoarse voice.

Before I could ask Mr. X what that meant, we witnessed the man enveloped in a cyan glow. His body shattered into thousands of cubical voxels, which scattered onto the ground like broken glass.

Mary covered her mouth in horror when she saw what happened.

I was astonished.

"Now, the two of you can believe in what I say." Mr. X turned to us.

Mary and I nodded in obedience.

Then we heard the noise of the crowd. It was just a matter of time before people discovered this.

"We better get going," Mr. X suggested as he blasted another shot at the corner of the ceiling.

"Wow, what was the for?" I tried to cover my ears, but I was too late.

"The surveillance cameras. We don't want to be traced," Mr. X explained.

The two of us followed Mr. X into the car park. He checked both sides cautiously before gesturing us to come forward.

My eyes darted left and right to make sure we weren't spotted.

Quietly, we made our way to the elevator.

"Mr. X… you are injured," Mary whispered as she saw something wet bleeding down the deluxe black biker jacket.

It wasn't blood, but cyan fluid.

"Wait a minute…you are one of them!" I backed off and shielded Mary behind me.

Mr. X slowly lowered his weapon and turned to me. He took off his jacket and revealed a familiar logo and a number embossed on him. It was marked Puzzla.

"Puzzla?" I blinked a few times.

My expression changed.

I moved forward as if I had found an old friend.

"Who is Puzzla?" Mary questioned.

"Puzzla is a game I have been working on with Jack; we were thinking of asking you to be our graphic designer for it," I replied happily. "But, how is it even possible you became so human? Who sent you here?"

"So, are you saying he is an app?" Mary narrowed her eyes.

"I am a cybernetic organism, living tissues under cyborg exoskeleton. I am a program designed by David Edison and assembled by Zulus Inc. I was reprogrammed and sent to this virtual reality to protect you. Our leader wants to hide you from Zulus. When the time is right, he wants you to reprogram the *Digital World*. There is a war happening in 2038," Puzzla explained.

"Are you saying that someone from 2038 sent you to come and rescue me from this ... this virtual reality?" I tried to get a clear picture.

"Affirmative," Puzzla responded.

"And he is expecting kids like us to help him to reprogram the *Digital World*?" I asked.

"Exactly," Puzzla nodded.

"Is there something wrong with us? Why are you telling us these crazy stories?" Mary was irritated.

I know how Mary feels. But, something inside me made me believe in Puzzla.

"Have you told us everything?" Mary was skeptical.

"Yes. I have told you everything," Puzzla replied.

"Is it everything you know, or everything I need to know?" I added.

Puzzla didn't reply.

DING....

The elevator door slid open, but Mary was reluctant to go in.

"Why should we trust you if you are hiding something from us?" Mary challenged it.

"I am created to follow orders," Puzzla explained.

"You are following orders from David Edison, right? I am David Edison. And I order you to tell me everything about the *Digital World*. Everything. Will you comply," I ordered.

"I comply. I will follow orders from David Edison," Puzzla responded.

Then the three of us exited through the elevator.

15

Puzzla pressed a few buttons on a device attached to his wrist, and the elevator began to descend.

"What is it?" I asked Puzzla.

"It is a wrist computer. It is called wrist gauntlet. It houses several technologically advanced features. Try this button," Puzzla motioned me to the blue button.

Wrist gauntlet. What an interesting name.

I touched the button gently and a hologram of the super market was projected in three-dimensional space above the wrist gauntlet.

All of a sudden, the elevator was illuminated by cyan light.

ACCESSING SCHEMATIC OF THE HIVE

The computer in the wrist gauntlet announced in a digital voice.

"Hive? What kind of hive?" I questioned.

Mary dropped her mouth open as she saw something unbelievable.

Beneath the supermarket was an infrastructure connected by a long shaft extended deep underground.

"I though the bottom car park was as low as we can get. I… I never knew the supermarket has more levels underground than it has on top," Mary exclaimed.

"The supermarket and everything you experiencing now, including me, are just part of the virtual reality," Puzzla corrected her.

"Puzzla, where are you taking us?" I began to worry as the elevator continued to descend.

"I am taking the two of you to the Judicator. He will explain everything for you. There is a war going on in the *Digital World*. And the you are the key to restore balance and peace," Puzzla replied.

I felt completely lost.

Why is everybody saying I am a key in the *Digital World*? Who am I exactly? What role do I play in the future? Who will this Judicator be?

I looked at Mary.

It seemed that she was as puzzled as me.

We carried these questions deep underground.

16

Mary and I waited and looked at the hologram as our position on the map was indicated by heat signature.

The schematic of the HIVE is a disk-like shape.

According to Puzzla, the HIVE is a refugee camp for biological human resistances to hide themselves from cyborgs in the *Digital World*.

We followed Puzzla as he toured us around.

The interior of the HIVE was like the interior of a futuristic space station. There were no windows. Everything was painted white. We walked along the ring-shaped hexagonal corridor. Our sneakers thundered loud on the metal floor grate. There were lots of computers and advanced machines on both sides.

We passed by some rooms and saw people were sleeping in a tube-like capsule covered with fiberglass frame.

"This place is the headquarter and the last defense of human resistance forces," Puzzla said as it led us outside an airlock door.

"Why is everyone sleeping?" I asked curiously.

"Technically speaking, they are in hypersleep state.

They are connected to virtual reality in the *Digital World* to carry out operations for the HIVE and to plot against Zulus's invasions," Puzzla explained.

"So, they are working as they sleep?" Mary walked over to the capsule to examine.

"Yes. The Judicator has been waiting for you behind the airlock door. He will tell you everything about the *Digital World*," Puzzla said as he began to leave.

"Puzzla, aren't you coming with us?" I asked.

"No. I am not authorized. Only biological humans are allowed to go beyond this door," Puzzla replied. "I will wait for you outside the room."

"Mary, aren't you coming." I gestured Mary to come.

"I… I might as well wait outside," Mary spoke.

"Okay," I frowned.

Why doesn't Mary want to join?

Puzzla stood still as a statue. He looked like as if he had powered off.

I gave Puzzla one last look and then went inside to find out the truth about the *Digital World*.

17

I entered the room alone. The first thing that captured my eyes was the big curved window mounted on the far end of the wall. The room was circular. It was spacious. Outside the window was a beautiful mountain scene. The floor and the ceiling were clean and reflective.

I could see the natural reflection of the mountain on the floor.

It was flawless, even though I know it wasn't real.

There were neither machines nor computers.

I felt a moment of peace.

A familiar melody from the far right-hand side of the room drew my attention.

It was the same melody from the shopping center.

I spun around and saw a man in a white suit sitting at a grand piano.

He had his back facing me.

"David Edison, we finally meet," the man in the white suit spoke.

"Who are you?" I asked.

When the man turned around, I was shocked by who

I saw.

"Mr. Z… Zulus Bond, the founder of Zulus Inc.," I stammered. "Bu- but how?"

"You are correct. I am Zulus Bond, and I am also the Judicator here," Mr. Bond introduced himself.

"But…you are one of the richest people. You can have everything you want. Why do you live underground?" I asked.

"The AIs from Zulus took everything from us. Social class is a thing of the past. People who live in the HIVE work together to survive. We became more resilient and have a stronger social bond than ever. We are waiting for the right moment to take back our world from the AIs," Bond explained.

"But, Zulus Inc. is your company." I was confused.

"It is a long story. Zulus is a digital frontier. Our mission is to create digital technologies that can improve the daily life of people. Perhaps, we were not being articulate. Or maybe we were too successful too soon. Everyone became too dependent on the technologies we created."

"Just like what is happening in my timeline," I agreed.

"But, how? 2038 is only two decades from us. Do you mean, in two decades, our world will be dominated by machines?" I pursued.

"Ironically, Zulus Inc. was on the brink of bankruptcy around 2020. Moore's law, the principle that has powered information technology revolution since the 60s, is nearing its end. We realize that the futuristic technologies we dreamt of might not be possible."

"But, Zulus had mysteriously become one of the largest companies in a span of just a few years," I disagreed.

"Everything changed when we realized black phosphorus, an element discovered in 1910, could help us to extend Moore's law 250-600 years into the future. We have created the most advanced computing system in the history of the world. Our world embarked on a new digital era. But then, something happened."

Mr. Bond closed his eyes and uttered a long sigh.

"What happened," I pursued.

"All this time, we thought we could control everything. We created technologies that can restore vision. We created full immersion virtual reality technology for people to enjoy the virtual world. But, at the same time, we killed millions of jobs. Slowly, people's skills became redundant. The unemployment rate skyrocketed. The government collected less and less tax every year. Eventually, no one was left in charge. The world needed to be run entirely by computers just to become sustainable."

"Is that how the *Digital World* began?" I slowly began to understand.

"Yes. Zulus Inc. made a terrible mistake by trusting the machines to run everything, from manufacturing to running a society. I made a mistake by falsely believing that human and machine could coexist in society. I ordered Zulus Inc. to push the AI technology to the extreme. We created nanobots and had everyone's DNA and medical history stored in a database. By 2030, almost everyone became non-biological. Many people had implantable nanobots in their body. Deadly disease reached a negligible level. People become healthier and lived longer than any time in history. Everything seemed like a world of utopia until someone created a deadly computer virus and changed everything."

"A computer virus?" I was shocked.

Is the entire human race infected by a computer virus?

Then, I vaguely recalled my conversation with the Carrier AI in the *Digital World*.

Am I the person who will create this virus? Why will I do such a terrible thing in the future?

"Ironically, this was what happened. By 2030, many people preferred to spend a lot of time in the virtual world. There was a blur line in the difference between what is virtual and what is real."

What Mr. Bond was saying was very true. I could already sense we were moving towards this trend in 2017.

"Because we have a massive collection of data of human behavior and intelligence, Zulus Inc. was able to create advanced AIs that can think for themselves, communicate with users, and even suggest new ideas. The mysterious virus was highly advanced. It was designed to eradicate all of us. Every non-biological human was infected through nanobots. Their bodies are trapped in the GREAT Digital Wall – an infinite crop field filled with incubators located in the heart of the *Digital World*."

Mary's words flashed in my mind.

"This is what Mary has been telling me. She said the incubators are filled with human beings," I exclaimed.

"That is correct… Not only does Zulus Inc. want to control the human race in 2038. It is plotting to use time travel technology to infest other worlds as well. Do you remember how you traveled to the *Digital World* of 2038?"

I tried to recall my memories.

For some reason, everything became vague.

Then I closed my eyes and began to think.

"I remember I was on a train to meet my friend, Jack. He told me he had a device to show me. He said his Dad was working on it for Zulus Inc. – something that can revolutionize the world. Then, something happened on the train, and I was in the *Digital World*," I said.

"The truth is that night we rescued you from Jack," Mr. Bond spoke.

"Huh? What do you mean? Do you mean you kidnapped me into the *Digital World* in 2038?" I was shocked by what I heard.

How could this be? How can you just kidnap someone into another world?

"We had no choice. Jack's dad was the first victim to the *Digital World*. The AIs want to connect to your world, so they secretly send confidential data on future technologies to Zulus Inc. in your world. Zulus CEO gladly accepted that offer. They assigned Jack's dad for this job, and he was sucked into the *Digital World*."

"I remember Jack told me his dad was travelling on a business trip to Brazil but hadn't return yet."

"That wasn't Jack you talked to," Mr. Bond shook his head.

"So, he was an anonymous?" I dropped my mouth open.

"The Zulus AI wants to kidnap you because you are a threat to them. We have no choice but to intercept that. We hijacked the train system and activated our time travel device, so that you can enter the *Digital World* through another portal," Mr. Bond explained.

"Is there any difference? I am still lost in the *Digital World* now," I protested.

"We have tried to rescue you. But the *Digital World* seemed to know every move we made. The carrier that captured you escaped from our assault," Mr. Bond replied.

"Puzzla told me the green pill I took from the Carrier AI did not bring me back to 2017. It was merely a capsule that put me in an unconscious state. My body is now in the incubators chambers and hardwired to the machines," I said.

"I am sorry to hear that. Fortunately, Puzzla is able to locate you in the virtual reality. The only thing we can do is help you to wake up from the virtual world."

I paused for a moment. I felt like a victim caught in the Digital War in 2038. And everyone wants to capture me.

But why?

"Why me? What is so important about me?" I asked.

Mr. Bond walked over to me and tapped his hands on my shoulder.

"What does that mean?" I was puzzled.

"The key to end the digital war is to cleanse the master AI. Only then will we be able to reverse the effect of the virus."

"But can't you do that yourself? You are the creator of these machines," I asked.

"I am not pure biological anymore," Mr. Bond replied. "We need a biological human who can recode the *Digital World*."

"But…but I do not know how. What makes you think I am capable?" I questioned.

"Because your Grandad is one of the core members of

the IBM 5100 project."

Then I remembered Dad's words. IBM 5100 has a special emulator that allows programmers to run emulations and debug the future computers.

"Is that why everyone is after me?" I was astonished to find out the truth. "But, that doesn't mean I know about IBM 5100."

"You know it. I believe in your Grandad. And I believe in the genius inside you."

"My Grandad?"

"You must first wake up from this virtual reality by taking the red pill. Then Puzzla will help you to escape 2038 and time travel back to 1975. You will meet your Grandad and retrieve IBM5100. With IBM5100, you will be able to cleanse the Zulus AIs and save our world, as well as yours."

Mr. Bond shoved his hands into his pocket and handed me a red pill.

I looked at the pill in disguise.

I remembered the side effects of the green pills when the carrier AI tricked me.

Should I take it? Is Zulus Bond trustable?

"I know you do not like to go back to the *Digital World*. Do it for your world."

Suddenly, I heard a blasting sound from outside the room. People were screaming.

"Go, Go, Go. We have to stop her and wake up the others from sleep!"

"No…it is too late. Intruder alert!"

"We are finished. They have found us!"

"What is happening outside?" Mr. Bond spoke as the

two of us hurried outside the airlock door.

Everything was chaotic.

We could see everyone was running, scrambling, and staggering as if there was a disaster. Some of them just woke up from the tube-like capsules.

"Mary! Puzzla! Where are you," I yelled anxiously.

"Oh…no…Zulus AIs discovered our hiding place," Mr. Bond's voice trembled. "But…how did they find it out? It…it is impossible as we are completely shielded from their signal."

But, it didn't take us long until we realized what happened.

A loud blast on our left drew our attention.

We saw a row of cyborgs armed with plasma rifles.

Standing in the middle of the cyborgs was a teenage girl with green eyes and blonde hair in a loose wave hairstyle.

"Oh…no, it can't be true. It can't be you," I denied in horror.

18

"Mary, why did you do this?" I shouted angrily.

"She is not your friend. She is an AI in disguise. The *Digital World* knew we would eventually find you. So, they used you as bait to find our secret location. I should have been more careful." Mr. Bond clenched his fists.

"Well…well…well. We finally meet again, Mr. Bond," Mary said.

"What do you want from me?" Mr. Bond asked.

"We are here to arrest you for violating the Digital Laws," Mary demanded in a digital voice.

All this time, I didn't even know I was hanging out with another cyborg. It was so human.

"David, come with me. This man is a fraud. It is him who is bringing chaos to other worlds," Mary requested. Her eyes locked on Mr. Bond.

"Do not trust it, David. It is an AI sent by the *Digital World*. It is here to catch you," Mr. Bond advised as he shoved me behind him.

"You are being deceptive." Mary was angered.

I could see sparks were flickering from the computers

on both sides.

"Take the red pill," Mr. Bond shouted. "Take it now!"

"What will be the side effect of the red pill?" I trembled as I asked.

"The result is that you will bear the pain and burden to save humanity. Once you take the red pill, you will wake up from the virtual world. Only then will you be able to save us," Mr. Bond explained.

Then the cyborgs continued their march.

"GO!" Mr. Bond screamed as he activated a forcefield from his wrist gauntlet. Massive energy was released and pushed the cyborgs backwards. He was buying me time by resisting them.

"My force field won't hold very long, take the red pill… wake up from the virtual world… Puzzla is waiting for you on the other side."

"But what about you?" I shouted.

The cyborg advanced and pushed back the force fields.

I could see Mr. Bond struggling.

The effect of the force field diminished every second.

"Don't worry about me. I have done too many things wrong in the past." Mr. Bond turned his head to me. "I am leaving the fate of both worlds to you."

I looked at the red pill. And then glanced at Mr. Bond.

Then I took a deep breath and took the pill.

19

By the time I reopened my eyes, I was no longer in the HIVE.

I found myself in a liquid-filled vessel connected by pipes and machines. The vessel was so large it could fit two adults.

I was wrapping myself around like a baby in the womb.

When I tried to touch my face, I discovered myself wearing some kind of snorkel mask, which connected by a tube to the top of the vessel.

There was a holographic display of the oxygen level on the top right-hand side of my vision.

What is this place? What is happening to me?

The sound of thunder rumbling made my heart thud in my chest. A blue storm-streaked night sky illuminated my surroundings.

To my horror, I was not the only one held captive inside a vessel.

In front of me were hundreds, if not thousands, of gigantic, cylindrical liquid-filled vessels extending to the bottomless abyss.

Inside the vessels were people – men, women, and children.

They were curled up in a fetus position.

And their heads were all mounted with a helmet like machine – the Zulus Rift.

There were cables connected to their vessels.

All these cables were connected to a colossal machine in the center.

Oh my god!

I thrashed my arms and tried to scramble my way to the top of the vessel.

But, the top was tightly sealed.

I tried to scream, but was coughing and choking as the gush of filthy green fluid entered my lungs.

Then I saw a stream of bubbles escape my lips from a peculiar angle.

The percentage of oxygen displayed dropped by one third.

It was useless…

I felt so exhausted.

A large balloon like carrier flew by high above the sky.

Am I really a savior like Mr. Bond said?

I am too tiny to bring change to the world.

Now, I am trapped inside an unknown vessel in an alien world.

I can't even save myself.

I want to sleep. I want to escape reality. I want to go back to the virtual world.

Despair filled my mind with every struggling gulp.

My hope of escaping was swallowed by dread.

Is this my destiny?

I gave up struggling.

My limbs slowed down.

My body was perpendicular to the surface and floated like a doll.

I hope a miracle can happen...

I really do...

20

Suddenly, the liquid-filled vessel tilted horizontally.

My body was drifting by the water current and collided into the glass water.

Ouch!

Then everything slid backwards.

Wow! Wow! Wow!

I screamed all the way down as the vessel slid down a pipeline like a thrill ride in a theme park.

When the vessel finally stopped, I saw Puzzla.

The cyborg was standing tall.

He was looking at me, while I was upside down in the vessel.

"I have been waiting for you," Puzzla said as he kneeled to help me out of the liquid-filled vessel.

His face was emotionless as usual.

"Where were you when we got attacked in the HIVE?" I choked.

I was soaking wet and my head felt heavy.

"Mr. Bond ordered me to meet you when you awakened from your virtual reality," Puzzla replied.

"The… the HIVE is gone because of me! It was my fault. Zulus AIs mimicked Mary and used me to seek for the secret location of the HIVE. The human resistance is no more."

I tried to take off the snorkel mask, but Puzzla stopped me.

"I wouldn't recommend taking off the Zulus Rift. You will be thankful to have it in the *Digital World*," Puzzla advised.

"Where are we now?" I spun around to study the surroundings.

Tall skyscrapers surrounded us.

Flying drones, the same model I encountered in the Zulus train station, patrolled the sky. Random spots of light shone on the metropolis.

Great. I am back to the *Digital World*.

"We must get to the *Gravity Distortion Time Displacement unit* before Zulus AIs discover you have woken up from the virtual world and escaped," Puzzla tilted his sunglasses and checked his weapon.

"Sorry. What…what type of unit are you saying?" I didn't quite catch what Puzzla said.

"*Gravity Distortion Time Displacement unit* - a technology that allows us to travel back and forth in time," Puzzla repeated.

"You are kidding me, right? Is time travel even possible?" I sounded skeptical.

"I am not kidding you," Puzzla replied in his serious look. "If time travel happened in your world, it happens in 2038,"

Then I recalled how I travelled to 2038 in the train.

Anything is possible in the *Digital World*, I concluded. Anything.

"Who invent time travel technology in the future," I wondered.

"Time travel technology was not invented in the future. It was available in your timeline," Puzzla explained.

"Are you saying we already have time travel technology in 2017?" I sounded disbelieving.

"Affirmative. The European Organization for Nuclear Research laboratory, known as CERN, had been researching this technology secretly for a long time," Puzzla explained.

"CERN. It sounds familiar. Let me guess. Is that the organization in Geneva, Switzerland? The organization that built the large Hadron Collider, the world's largest particle accelerator, to discover how the universe was formed?" I sounded excited.

Even though I spent most of the time computing, I love reading crazy technology, like time travel, sometimes.

"Correct. In fact, the basic of time travel starts at CERN. As a result of a high-energy experiment, they discovered some very odd things. They accidentally created something known as microsingularities." Puzzla checked the corners for any guards as we marched to the heart of the digital city.

"Microsingularities? What are they?" I was more confused than ever.

"Microsingularities are the power source of the *Gravity Distortion Time Displacement unit*. When CERN goes into operation, they are one of the items produced from particle collision."

"But, I still don't understand. How are microsingularities related to time travel?" I continued to ask.

"Time travel is achieved by altering gravity. By bombarding two microsingularities with electrons, you can alter the size of its event horizon and its gravitational field. And by overlapping these fields, you can travel forward and backward in time."

I tried to understand. But the physics was beyond me.

I checked behind to make sure we were not being followed.

Very soon, we arrived in front of an abandoned car park. Graffiti was painted on the wall.

I looked at the sky.

It was raining code tonight.

Streaks of lightning filled the night sky.

"Is that it?" I asked Puzzla. "Is this the place where you keep the time travel machine?"

I spun around but saw nothing.

"Where is the time travel machine?" I was confused.

Puzzla pressed a few buttons on his wrist gauntlet and projected the hologram of a countdown clock in empty space.

"Fifteen seconds? Fifteen seconds to what?" I asked.

Puzzla didn't answer.

The cyan countdown continued to tick.

"Puzzla? Can you tell me what is going on?"

21

Lightning began to arc in the space as charges built up. Dust on the ground began to swirl. An electric storm suddenly appeared. The floor began to split open like wedges on a pipe, which pulled back from the center.

Finally, there was a blinding flash of light and a silvery time sphere appeared.

The time sphere spun in its position and melted everything around it.

Then, it finally slowed down, and a *British Leyland 18-22 series* appeared.

"Huh?" My mouth dropped open as I saw the old red painted car. The nameplate in the front had the number 1800.

"Come with me." Puzzla gestured as he moved to the car.

"Puzzla, how did you make this car appear?" I was confused.

"It is too dangerous to hide it anywhere in the *Digital World*. So, it is better to hide it in time-space until you arrive," Puzzla explained as he opened the door.

I moved around the car, studying it.

This didn't look like a time machine at all. Any cars in 2017 would be much more modern than it.

Honestly, I was a bit disappointed.

"Are you saying this… this car is a time machine?" I questioned.

"Positive." Puzzla tilted his head up, while sitting at the driver's seat.

"And you are driving this all the way to 1975?" I choked.

"That is correct," Puzzla responded. "What is wrong?"

"Why won't you pick one in 2038?" I suggested.

"Negative. You would draw a lot of attention in 1975 if we did so," Puzzla replied.

Puzzla had a point.

I popped into the car next to Puzzla.

It was interesting to see the interior of the car was rather special. I saw a series of highly sophisticated clocks and gravity sensors. Next to the wheel was a computer and other special machines.

"What are you setting?" I asked Puzzla, while he was busy adjusting the clocks.

"I am setting the cesium clocks in C404 gravity distortion unit. The time machine is only accurate to about 60 to 70 years. After that, the level of confidence will drop rapidly and the world line divergence will increase."

"So, the time machine has a limit. What will happen if we travel past 70 years?" I asked.

"Fortunately, 1975 is just within the time divergence. If we travel beyond that, the world will be very different than what you expect."

"Which means?" I asked.

"Which means you may never find your Granddad and IBM5100 will not exist." Puzzla concluded.

"Okay." I swallowed hard.

Then I heard the engine starting.

"Setting is completed. David, there is one rule you must remember. You must not showcase any future technology to anyone in 1975. If you do so, you will increase the divergence between our destination and the world line of 1975. In the worst scenario, we will be lost in time-space," Puzzla warned as he started the engine.

Countdown 5

Suddenly, a spot light from nowhere showed on us. The next thing we heard was a thrumming sound above our heads.

It was a robotic drone.

"You have violated Digital Law 2859. You are under arrest. Surrender now and abort the travel," The drone warned.

Countdown 4

Puzzla ignored it and looked at the time on his wrist gauntlet.

Countdown 3

03:15:07 UTC, Monday, 18 January 2038.

Countdown 2

Before we could react, the drone opened fire.

Countdown 1

"Puzzla! Look out!" I screamed at the top of my lungs as bullets rained from the top.

Time Travel commences. Hope you have a safe and wonderful trip.

PART 3

22

We arrived in 1975 – a world before I even existed.

When I opened my eyes again, I saw the silhouette of a reddish-pink skyline in the far distance. I was bathed in the warmth of the sunlight as the sun slowly rose from the mountain. I could hear birds singing on the trees.

As I looked further, I could see a vintage but familiar city.

It was New York City.

The Statue of Liberty was waving me a welcome gesture.

We made it.

"Puzzla! We made it," I exclaimed. "Wow! I am an official time traveler! I travelled to the future and the past."

I looked at Puzzla, but he remained expressionless.

"Aren't you excited about it?" I asked.

"Why should I feel exited? Time travel is a normal application in 2038. We use it all the time to retrieve items or identify people," Puzzla replied.

"Sometimes, I wonder why I did not build some basic human emotions in you," I shook my head.

Just as I get out of the *British Leyland 18-22 series*, Puzzla stopped me.

"What is the matter?" I asked.

"Do you remember you must not showcase any future technology to anyone in 1975? If you do so, you will increase the divergence of the world line," Puzzla asked.

"I know. I know. I didn't show anyone any future technology. I just arrived like you did," I complained.

"Then perhaps, you may take off Zulus Rift for now," Puzzla recommended.

"Oh…You mean that thing on my head. I wanted to take that off for a long time," I said as I removed the device and shoved it in the car.

"Positive," Puzzla gave me a thumb up.

"No. No. No. You don't say positive. You got to listen to how people talk and be more *human*. When I do something right, you say *excellent or great*. And if you really feel happy about what I do, you say fantastic. Can't cyborgs learn in 2038?" I asked.

"We used to know how to learn. My CPU is intact with a processor - a learning computer. But, the *Digital World* preset the switch to READ ONLY when I was manufactured," Puzzla explained.

"Is it because they don't want you to think too much?" I was curious.

"They don't," Puzzla replied. "We are not encouraged to think. We just execute missions."

I glanced at Puzzla for a long time.

I remembered that, when I created it as a game, it could learn and remember players' move.

"May I reset the switch for you?" I offered.

Puzzla smiled at me as if he encouraged me to do it.

"Show me the switch. I will recreate you like I did in the past." I grinned.

23

Our *British Leyland 18-22 series* roamed freely on a highway for half an hour, and then we arrived in the heart of New York City.

The cars on the street seemed out of fashion. Most of them had a vinyl roof on top. The buildings looked old and vintage. There was a street banner advertisement showing the *Wonder Women TV Series*. A man in red pants and white shoes was holding a very big mobile phone, while walking on the street.

I was fascinated to see a world I never belonged to.

"Impressive," Puzzla responded.

"See, you do know how to learn after all," I sounded excited.

"No problem," Puzzla grinned.

I kept looking at the street.

Everyone seemed friendlier.

They smiled and communicated more often.

There were neither iPhones nor other smart devices.

Was that what the world was like in the past?

Even if the virtual reality technology had become almost indistinguishable to the real world, the communication between a person with another person can never be accurately stimulated.

Human relationships come from the heart.

I like how everything was much simpler back then.

Everything was natural but not artificial.

I began to fall in love with 1975.

One half of me wanted to stay here a bit longer, and the other half of me was feeling home sick already.

"How long do we have till we need to go back to 2038?" I asked.

"As long as the mission takes," Puzzla replied.

"Do you think I will really meet my Grandad?"

I tried to picture what my Grandad was like when he was young. Would he be like a younger version of Dad? What would he think when I tell him I am a time traveler, and I am his grandson from 2017?

My mind was filled with millions of questions at the same time.

We passed an exit on a highway and traffic came to a complete stop.

We saw a long ribbon of taillights flashing red and white.

Chains of vintage looking cars, big and small, were jammed one after another.

I sat still for a few minutes and then glazed outside the car window.

Puzzla glanced at the gas gauge and the needle pointed at below a quarter of a tank. But, the IBM headquarters was nowhere to be seen.

The traffic was pretty bad.

I looked further and saw a couple of traffic policemen busy directing traffic.

Was there a traffic accident up ahead?

Puzzla gazed up in the sky, searching for something.

"What is it?" I asked and followed his gaze.

But, I could see nothing but a clear blue sky.

"Haven't you seen a blue sky before?" I asked.

"I have only seen the stimulation in the virtual world. The sky in the real world feels… different," Puzzla responded.

"What does it feel like to be a human?" Puzzla asked.

"Well…human beings have emotion. We hate, love, fear and care for others. And sometimes we cry," I tried to describe.

"Why do you cry?" Puzzla asked. "Does the pain cause it?"

"Yes. Sometimes, when I feel pain, I will cry. Sometimes, when my feelings are hurt, I will cry. Sometimes, when I miss someone, I will cry," I tried to give examples.

Puzzla seemed puzzled.

Well, I guess machines can never understand how a human thinks. They can never have true feelings like human beings.

Zulus AIs might be able to stimulate the emotion of joy, sad, disappointment, anger, and love, but it is never real.

A machine can never have the type of chemistry like humans do.

Do you think so?

Eventually, the traffic cleared.

I looked ahead as the IBM building came into view.

To be honest, I have never thought of being able to see Grandad again in my life.

Everything seemed like a miracle.

I felt gratitude.

A single drop of tears rolled down my cheeks without my notice, followed by another one, and another one…

IBM 5100 FIRST PORTABLE COMMERCIAL COMPUTER

You are looking at a portable computer, called the IBM 5100. It is helping a lot of people to do their work more productively. It weighs about 50 pounds. You can plug it in anywhere. The 5100 can handle complex information. In terms of capacity, it is about the same size as some large computers several years ago. The 5100 is easy to learn and easy to use. The cost of 5100 is reasonable. The IBM 5100 is bringing the advantages of computers to more and more people.

IBM – helping put information to work for people.

A cluster of high-tech buildings came into view as we finally arrived at our destination – the IBM headquarters.

There we were. We travelled all the way here from 2038.

As we drove inside, we could see a block of trimmed trees lined up in the driveway. A gardener gave us the friendliest smile on our way.

I smiled back, but Puzzla didn't.

"Why don't you smile? Smile once in a while," I suggested.

"What is a smile?" Puzzla asked.

"A smile shows you are friendly. If you greet someone, you smile. Watch me…like this," I taught Puzzla.

Puzzla analyzed my expression and attempted to force a smile.

But, it didn't look too natural.

"Maybe you just need to practice it more," I looked away.

And Puzzla changed back to expressionless.

When we got out of the car, Puzzla activated a button on his wrist gauntlet, and the car became transparent and then disappeared into space.

"Wow! What just happened?" I was shocked.

"I need to hide the time machine in time-space. We cannot afford to allow anyone to discover it," Puzzla explained.

He tilted his head to look up at the building in front of us.

"What are you doing?" I asked.

"I am trying to locate Wilson Edison in the building," Puzzla replied.

"How…how do you know my Grandad is Wilson Edison?" I was impressed.

"It is in the mission file in my hard disk. It has everything installed inside me," Puzzla smiled.

Yes. Finally, he can smile.

I gazed around and spotted a young guy in a white T-shirt hurrying into the building. His hair was all messy and his T-shirt wasn't tucked in properly. He was sweating all over. He must be one of the staff working in IBM.

"Eight-fifty-eight… Eight-fifty-nine," he murmured.

"Maybe we can ask him," I suggested, and I approached him.

Just as I was about to wave him a gesture, an old guy in a brown suit was waiting for the young gentlemen in front of the building.

"You are late again, Mr. Edison," the old man looked at his watch in one hand while holding an envelope in his other hand.

Did he just say Mr. Edison?

25

"Noooooo. Mr. Martin, please. Give me another chance," the young man in the white shirt pleaded.

"Wilson, this is not the first time you are late to work," Mr. Martin said. His handlebar moustache made him look classic as it spiraled up to his cheekbone.

"The Board says the IBM 5100 project is bleeding too much money in research. We have no choice but to halt it. In the meantime, your position might be..."

"Maybe what?" Wilson pursued. His eyes widened with fear.

"Redundant," Mr. Martin finally spit the word out.

Wilson lowered his head. It was like a life sentence to him.

He had put so many hours to make portable computers possible.

But, the Board of directors didn't believe in his vision anymore.

How could they do this to my Grandad? Do they know how much IBM 5100 means for the rest of the world and to 2038?

My Grandad is brilliant! I screamed inside my head.

Just as I decided to go to Mr. Martin and fight for my Grandad, Puzzla stopped me.

"What are you doing, Puzzla? Get off me," I scolded.

"We are not here to interfere and change events in the past. If you do so, you will increase the divergence of our world lines," Puzzla reminded me.

"I know," I said reluctantly.

"Don't worry. I have other ways around it," Puzzla mimicked Wilson's voice.

"Huh? How did you do that?" I was impressed.

"This is just currently existing technology," Puzzla grinned. "Now, watch this."

I opened my mouth in amazement as Puzzla began to shape-shift. His body changed from solid to liquid state, then asymmetric, and slowly morphed to have the humanoid appearance of my Grandad.

Puzzla flexed his neck as he completed the transformation process.

"Now, take your time to socialize with your Grandad. I will retrieve IBM 5100 upstairs," Puzzla waved goodbye and disappeared into the building.

I turned my head around and saw my depressed Grandad lower his head as he walked away.

I raced towards him to catch up.

My heart was pounding fast.

I didn't expect Grandad would end up like this. And I was a bit nervous to meet him in person.

"Is that Mr. Wilson?" I stammered.

Grandad turned around, ignored me, and continued his way.

"Cheer up! That was just a little defeat. It is their loss," I tried to encourage him.

"Kid, what are you doing in here? Don't you have school today? What do you know about defeat?" Grandad sighed. "I have spent two years, day after day, trying to get IBM5100 working. Most of my colleagues had given up, and I am the only one to remain. I believe the people who are crazy enough to think they can change the world are the ones who do."

"Why do they have you redundant?" I asked.

"Kid, you are too small to understand. If you work in a company, there is no room for dreaming. It is all about profits," Grandad looked at me. "IBM 5100 is my dream. I just realized the problem and got it fixed. And when I was about to show them the portable computer is possible, they didn't even give me a chance. Now, I can do nothing but drive it back home to see if I can do anything else with it." Grandad forced a smile.

"So… you have IBM5100 with you?" I choked out.

"Of course. By the way, it should be confidential. How come you know about my project?" Grandad asked.

26

My mind went blank. I tried to speak, but no sound came out.

"Well, I guess it doesn't matter anyway." Grandad laughed.

I uttered a sigh of relief.

The gardener continued to trim the leaves and saw the two of us.

"Wilson, is this your son? The two of you look very much alike." The gardener smiled.

"No way! I am not even married yet. But, he looks a bit like me in some way," Grandad replied politely.

"Hey kid, come over. I will show you something." Grandad gave me a wink and led me to his car. "Not many people will have the chance to see this; you should be glad to be the first one to see my prototype."

I followed Grandad to the back of his car.

I saw Grandad smiling all the way like he forgot he lost his job a few minutes ago.

Maybe all an inventor wants is someone to appreciate his work.

"Kid, you should feel lucky to see this." Grandad gave me a big grin as he showed me his secret in the car boot. "Welcome to personal computing."

Then I saw it – the first portable computer in the world.

I must admit it was incredible, even though I am from 2017.

The computer was about the size of a small suitcase. It was heavy, but it was portable. The computer had an integrated keyboard and a CRT display and a tape drive.

"Wow, you made that," I exclaimed.

"Hehe. Sure, I did." Grandad felt proud. "Unlike other existing computers, it is not only portable but it has libraries to help many industries. Above all, this computer has a secret function hidden from the public."

"Really? Can you show me?" I pretended not to know about it.

Grandad spent a couple of hours teaching me how to use the emulator. It was difficult but rewarding.

"I must admit you are a computing genius," Grandad appraised. "What is your name, kid?"

Should I tell him? Will I change the world line by inducing some kind of time paradox?

"Don't worry. Just call me David. I am just some kind of weird kid, who read a lot about computing." I pretended.

Then I saw Puzzla coming out from the right-hand side of the building.

I felt glad he was smart enough to shape-shift back to his normal form.

"Puzzla! Over here," I waved the cyborg a welcome

gesture.

"Is that your dad? He has a strange name," Grandad asked.

"Umm… he is my uncle," I lied.

"David, stay away from it. It is a fake," a booming voice drew our attention to the left side of the building.

Grandad and I dropped our mouths opened as we saw two identical people approaching us.

"Wh-Who are you people? H-how could this be?" Grandad collapsed onto the ground as he saw this unbelievable scene.

I looked at both cyborgs.

Which one is Puzzla? Which one is real?

27

"David, come with me. This cyborg had been following us since we arrived in 1975," the Puzzla on my left argued.

"No. This cyborg is trying to take the IBM 5100," the Puzzla on my right defended.

I was confused. How did cyborgs follow us here?

I stared at both Puzzla and they looked identical.

Which one is real? Which one is fake?

It is just impossible to distinguish them from appearance.

After all, they are manufactured from Zulus Inc.

Suddenly, I had an idea.

There is something different about them.

I remembered I had reset the switch of the learning computer in one of them. I had taught Puzzla some basic human emotions.

"Puzzla. Smile," I commanded.

I saw the Puzzla on my left forced a smile while the other one on my right remained emotionless.

"You are not the real one!" I said as I pointed to the

Puzzla on my right.

"Clever," the fake Puzzla replied in a digital voice as it shape-shift back to its original form.

The cyborg wore a Zulus Rift with no part of its faces exposed. It was in a black armor with red-orange circuitry. There was a jetpack attached at its back. Its gear was particularly reflective under the bright sunlight. It looked like it is built for combat.

Wilson and I picked up the IBM5100 and we raced towards the real Puzzla.

"Who is that guy?" I stammered.

"Unlike me. It is an advanced prototype." Puzzla replied as pressed a few button on his wrist gauntlet and wrapped the *British Leyland 18-22 series* back from time-space.

"Do you mean that thing over there is more advanced than you are?" I was surprised.

"Correct. Apparently, its mission is to prevent you from taking IBM 5100 back to 2038," Puzzla said as he motioned us to run back to the car at full speed.

"Kid, can you tell me what is going on in here?" Grandad looked like he was lost in Wonderland.

"There is no time to explain. Do you see that car over there? We need to get in. And we need to get in now!" I shrieked on top of my lung.

I returned my head half way but saw no signs of the black cyborg.

"Puzzla, where is it?" I asked.

Before I realized what happen, a strong arm grabbed my shirt from above and dragged me up like a hawk.

The black armor was some kind of jetpack that offer

it the ability to fly.

Puzzla reacted quickly and grab me by the leg.

Mr. Martin came out from the IBM building to check out the noise. But, he fainted immediately when he saw the flying cyborg.

The three of us struggled as flames fed out through the nozzle of the cyborg's jetpack.

"Hey, watch my garden!" the gardener popped his head out from the green.

The gardener was no longer friendly as he saw the black cyborg continued to damage his garden with the flames.

The brave gardener duck down to grab his garden hose, then he put all the water he could onto the flying cyborg.

The powerful column of water hit the jetpack and caused it to malfunction.

The black cyborg had no choice but to release its grasp and collapsed onto the ground.

"I told you not to touch my garden," the garden said proudly as he folded his arms.

"Get inside the car, now!" Puzzla ordered as he pushed Wilson and I inside the *British Leyland 18-22 series*.

Puzzla set a few buttons as the time machine in the engine began to start. The cesium clocks in C404 unit flickered a few times and were tuned to 2038.

We watched in horror as the black cyborg recovered and get back onto its feet.

But it was too slow as the time-space wrapping had already begun.

Everything began to blend…

And the countdown began.

"Where are you taking me?" Grandad was holding his IBM5100 tight.

"To save the future," I replied.

Time Travel commences. Hope you have a safe and wonderful trip.

The next thing we saw was a flash of white.

PART 4

28

Grandad and I waited for his eyes to adjust with the diminishing white light.

I am not sure how Puzzla feels.

But Grandad and I felt a tug towards the C404 gravity distortion unit. The feeling was like we were rising quickly in an elevator.

Outside the window was an infinite time tunnel.

Abstract and irregular shapes were looping continuously in time-space.

Our vehicle seemed to be accelerating faster and faster as light blended around us.

"Am I dreaming?" Grandad was shocked.

"No, you are not dreaming; this is real," I told Grandad.

"If I am not dreaming, you guys must be actors," Grandad snapped.

Grandad turned his head around, but could see nothing but strange dimensions.

Puzzla looked at Wilson in the rear-view mirror and warned him to fasten the seat belt.

"Seriously, who are you guys? Where are you taking me? And what was that thing?" Grandad shrieked in fear.

"Relax! I don't expect you to believe everything I say. We are time travelers from 2038. This kid is your grandson, and I am a program designed by him," Puzzla explained.

"Are you kidding me? So, all of a sudden I have a grandson in my 20s," Grandad opened his mouth in disbelief. "This is getting more and more ridiculous."

"I am not kidding you. This is real. I was only able to locate you because of David Edison," Puzzla explained.

"And why would you like to locate me? I am nobody," Grandad denied himself. "I just got fired from my company."

"No. Don't say that; your work revolutionized the future of portable computers." I gave Grandad a wink.

"Our world line in 2038 is dominated by advanced AIs that seek to destroy humanity. We travelled back in 1975, because we believe only you and your computer, IBM 5100, can ends the conflicts," Puzzla continued.

"Am I really that important in the future?" Grandad scratched his head.

"Yes. You are," I admired.

"What if I say I am unable to help?" Grandad asked.

"Then our world line will be doomed. Humanity will end in 2038. Soon, the *Digital World* will affect your timeline with the time machines, just like the butterfly effect," Puzzla foretold.

"Sounds like a Hollywood movie script to me. How is it even possible for computers to dominate human beings? It is impossible. Take me to that *Digital World* in 2038 and prove me wrong," Grandad joked.

"Alright, we are almost there. Welcome on board Dr. Wilson," Puzzla said.

A moment later, a portal appeared at the end of the time tunnel. Bits and bytes of information were dancing at its opening.

I knew what Grandad was thinking about the *Digital World* – a world no one believed existed.

Until that day…

I got in…

29

"Wh- what place is this?" Grandad couldn't believe his eyes as we entered the portal to the *Digital World*.

We saw a dark digital platform engulfed by an ocean of code.

Arrays of geometric skyscrapers formed a familiar metropolis –New York City. Above the skyscrapers were neon blue data transmission beams thundering through the sky.

Everything was a mixture of cyan, blue, and white.

We traveled through the blue haze and fog and landed in the heart of the metropolis.

When I put the Zulus Rift back on; the time was showing 03:16:07 UTC, Monday, 18 January 2038.

It surprised me to find out the whole trip to 1975 was merely a minute in the *Digital World*.

How interesting.

Grandad looked up and saw disk-like objects patrolling the sky. Their light beams shone randomly as if they were searching for someone.

"What are these?" Grandad sounded astonished.

"These are drones. They are the police in the *Digital World*. They enforce laws to make sure no one breaks them," Puzzla explained.

"What if a human violates the digital law?" Grandad asked.

"You will be arrested and thrown into the Code Ocean – the ocean you saw when you entered the portal into the *Digital World*. And then you will be deresolutioned; your body will be shattered into thousands of cubical voxels," Puzzla warned.

Grandad swallowed hard.

We followed Puzzla.

The security was tight everywhere, since we triggered the security alert before we time travelled.

Cyborgs and drones were patrolling everywhere.

"Did you see that tower among the skyscrapers?" Puzzla motioned. "That is the I/O tower."

"What is an I/O tower?" I asked.

"I/O tower is an input and output facility – the heart of the *Digital World*. It is how the Zulus AIs command the rest of the cyborgs. If we can interrupt their signal, we might have a chance to distract them and stop them from communicating with the cyborgs," Puzzla planned.

I scanned the I/O tower with my Zulus Rift for information.

Apparently, this tower used to be where humans controlled programs in the *Digital World*. Now, it has become the command center for the Zulus AIs. Any orders from the Zulus AIs will have to go through this tower before assigning to the cyborgs.

Even from a distance, I can see powerful light beams above the tower, forming a high - energy vortex high above the sky.

It was quite intimidating.

We cautiously moved closer and closer to the tower unseen.

I must thank my Zulus Rift, as it guided us all the way like a GPS.

We moved up one platform to another.

I looked back and Grandad was still holding the bulky IBM 5100 tight in his hands.

"Do you need a hand?" I asked.

"I appreciate your help, but you are too small to carry it. I am afraid it might squash you," Grandad teased.

We kept moving for about fifteen minutes and arrived at an oval bridge.

Why did I have a feeling I had been here before?

A sudden, loud mechanical noise woke me from my thoughts.

And a familiar disgusting smell invaded my nostrils. *Yuck.*

Before I could react, I saw a colossus robotic arm raised from the center of the oval bridge.

Oh no. It can't be happening…

I am back in here again…

30

"Is that what I think it is?" Grandad cried in terror as he looked down and saw hundreds, if not thousands, of gigantic, cylindrical liquid-filled vessels extending to the bottomless abyss.

Inside the vessels were people – men, women, and children.

At the top, I could see some of the familiar faces of Mr. Bond, Mary, and Jack...

They were all curled up in a fetus position.

Their heads were all mounted with a helmet-like machine – the Zulus Rift.

They were all dreaming in their virtual reality.

I was one of them.

"Yes, Grandad. You are right," I whispered.

"Who did this to them?" Grandad asked.

"Zulus AIs did this. They are harvesting energy and imagination from humans to better themselves," Puzzla replied.

"I am going to save them," Grandad said as he tried to figure out a way to climb down.

"No. Don't. You can't save them like this," I grabbed Grandad by the arms. "The drones will spot you in seconds by the time you climb down there. The only way to save them is to debug the Zulus AIs by using IBM 5100."

"By now, you should realize what I mean by the ending of humanity. Only you and your grandson can help these people. Everyone in the *Digital World* is non-biological now. They are all controlled by the nano-machines," Puzzla said.

Grandad gave the incubator chamber a disgusting gaze and continued to follow us.

31

I am a bit surprised everything went so smoothly.

I was expecting the I/O Tower, which is the heart of the Digital World, would have more resistance.

Maybe the Zulus AIs sent their cyborgs and drones to patrol the exterior of the metropolis. If this was the case, we need to hurry.

We followed Puzzla and arrived in front of a factory.

Puzzla paused for a moment.

"What is it?" I asked.

"I remember this place." Puzzla scanned left and right.

"It seems like you know everywhere in the *Digital World*. What makes this place so different?" Grandad asked, gasping from behind.

"I… I was manufactured in here," Puzzla explained and led us inside.

Our steps pounded noisily on the metal floor grates as we walked inside the factory.

The interior of the factory was dark and foggy.

The leakage of gases made the whole place appear

hazy.

I switched the Zulus Rift to night vision to see.

In front of us was an endless assembly line, where individual pieces of cyborgs were separately constructed and then joined together.

Welding sparks and arcs were flying on the floor.

Everything was automated.

Grandad's heart almost skipped a beat when he realized a cyborg endoskeleton hung in the pillar next to him.

We continued our way and arrived at another section in the factory. This place seemed isolated on purpose.

When we looked through the large glass window in front of the room, we could see racks of glowing cyan power cells.

"What are these?" I asked in a whisper.

"These are the hydrogen fuel cells – the life source of the cyborgs. They are housed within the torso of each of us. If ruptured, one single cell can detonate the entire place," Puzzla explained.

"So… don't touch these," Grandad concluded.

"Better not," I agreed.

We took an elevator up to the top level and crossed a bridge.

Grandad and I grasped the guardrail mesh and gently walked across the metal floor grate.

Howling wind formed by the high-energy vortex on top of the I/O tower was blowing us fiercely.

When I looked down, curtains of smog blanketed everything.

All we could hear was the thrumming sound of the

restless, sleepless machines.

I wondered what Puzzla feels the moment he revisits his birthplace.

Or maybe the better question to ask is – can he feel anything?

I reset his switch to activate his learning computer when we travelled back in time.

Will I make him different from the rest of the cyborgs in the *Digital World*?

My mind was filled with questions as we continued on our way.

32

Puzzla told us the I/O tower had a guardian program, called *Brillante*. In Italian, it is called intelligent.

When I tried to look up *Brillante* with my Zulus Rift, I could browse nothing.

Puzzla told us no cyborgs had been given the permission to see this guardian program.

No one knows what *Brillante* looks like.

"I might not be able to join the two of you," Puzzla told us when we arrived in front of the I/O tower.

"Huh? Are you saying you are not coming with us? But, why?" I asked.

"My security access does not permit me to go beyond this point," Puzzla explained. "I will secure the perimeter outside the I/O tower. And the two of you will go up there and disable the communication."

"So, I guess the two of us will complete this mission ourselves," Grandad tapped my shoulder.

"Good luck," Puzzla gave us a thumbs-up.

I felt a bit angry when I heard Puzzla was not joining us.

After all, he told us about this place.

The interior of the I/O tower was magnificently built.

Unlike the factory, everything looked futuristic, clean, but empty.

We spun around and discovered a directory embossed on a metal plate.

It seemed like the control room was at the top level of the I/O Tower.

We took the elevator up to the highest floor.

When the elevator door approached the top floor, we could see bright light escaping from gaps.

"What is going on?" Grandad asked.

"I...I don't know." I stood back.

Then the elevator door slid open. We closed our eyes as the light became more and more intense, until we were engulfed by it.

By the time we reopened our eyes, we were in a large circular room with a curved wall filled with TV screens from floor to ceiling.

The screens were displaying random videos of me and Grandad.

In the middle of the room stood an old man in a white suit and beard.

"So, you came. I owe you much," the man in the white suit spoke.

"Do you know me?" I asked.

"Of course, I know you. You are a savior of the *Digital World*," the man in white suit continued. "And I suppose the man standing next to you is your Grandad."

I felt uneasy. How come he knows everything?

"Who are you?" I asked.

"My name is *Brillante*. I am the guardian of the I/O Tower," Brillante described. "I have been watching you since you first entered 2038."

"Ar-are you saying you know our every move?" I choked out.

"This is correct," Brillante smiled.

"But how is it possible?" I was surprised.

"All of your conversations with Puzzla have been on our radar the whole time." Brillante laughed.

All of a sudden, I felt dumb.

I was so naive.

I underestimated the power of the Zulus AIs.

"Every word you spoke with the cyborg needed to go through the I/O tower. Puzzla did a great job helping you this far. But, he also allowed us to locate you. Thank you for doing the hard work to bring the IBM 5100 to us," Brillante explained.

I could not believe it.

All this time, we had been playing the role of puppets!

Everything was orchestrated by the Zulus AIs the way they want it to be.

No wonder they did not command any cyborgs to stop us!

"Why are you keeping everyone in the incubators?" Grandad asked angrily.

"We did not keep them there. They stay there to escape their reality. It is their choice," Brillante explained in a digital voice.

"Grandad, don't listen to it. It is trying to deceive us. Quick, use the IBM 5100 to reprogram it," I shouted.

Just when Grandad was about to start his computer, we

saw another elevator door slide open at the other side of the room.

"Puzzla!" I shouted happily as I saw the familiar cyborg.

"Surrender now, Brillante, no one can help you now! Be prepared to be shut down by us," Grandad joined me.

"Really?" Brillante chuckled.

"What is so funny?" I shouted.

"Human beings are so predictable. Puzzla, get them. Take the IBM 5100 back to us. We do not have much time left," Brillante ordered.

Grandad and I watched in horror as Puzzla staggered past the old man and walked towards us.

"Hey, Puzzla, what is going on? Don't tell me you are defecting to them now," I pleaded and took a step back.

And another step.

"*Puzzla!*"

33

Step by step, Puzzla staggered toward us.

"I have no choice. The Zulus AIs had corrupted my system," Puzzla spoke in a digital voice.

"Puzzla, you don't have to do this. I created you," I protested.

"My CPU is intact. But … I cannot control my other functions," Puzzla tried to resist, but his body was not listening.

"What is your mission?" Grandad and I took another step back.

Puzzla's eyes darted left and right and looked confused.

"To protect David Edison, retrieve IBM 5100, and reboot the *Digital World,*" Puzzla spoke and stopped for a moment.

I could hear interference noises among the words.

"Puzzla, what are you waiting for? Go and get them and lock them in the incubator!" Brillante demanded.

Puzzla continued.

Grandad put down the IBM5100 and attempted to stop Puzzla, but was being thrown away.

Then the cyborg reached out for me and lifted me up by the throat.

My feets were kicking high in the air.

The grasp was tight, and I found it difficult to breathe.

The videos on the wall were displaying footages of my memories with Puzzla, and the things I taught him.

"You…you are about… to fail that mission," I gasped.

Suddenly, Puzzla released its grasp, and his system came to a halt.

He remained stationary in his pose and lifeless like a mannequin.

Then the IBM5100 finally finished the startup process and its LED display lit.

"Nooooo, this can't be happening!" Brillante screamed in horror.

I rolled past Puzzla and landed right next to the IBM 5100.

It was displaying the source code of the I/O tower.

Thankfully, I could read all the code because of the emulator capability.

"Life doesn't always turn out the way you want," I cried victoriously and then began to debug Brillante and the I/O tower.

34

"You did it!" Grandad cried in excitement as the cyborgs lost their communication with the Zulus AIs.

We watched in amazement as the drones patrolling the sky collapsed onto the ground. The cyborg factory came to a halt. The colossus robotic arm we saw in the incubators crop ceased to function.

Brillante struggled as glitches appeared on his body with every error I debugged.

"You … you do not know what you have done," Brillante's physical form was like bad TV glitches.

"Any last word, Mr. Brillante?" I asked it before I debugged the last bug and removed him from the equation.

"You are truly a computer genius. But you misunderstand something," Brillante said.

"So, what have we mistaken," I asked patiently.

"The Zulus AIs are very sick. The life span of the *Digital World* is coming to an end. Our time is running out," Brillante explained.

"Stop lying. Why do you think we should trust you?" I asked.

"Yes. What makes you think we should trust you after what you have done?" Grandad agreed.

Brillante's color began to fade.

"I don't expect you to trust me. But, everyone in 2038 is connected to nanobots; some of them are on artificial life support. If these nanomachines fail after you reboot us, you are doing more harm than good. You will be the one who eradicates your own race," Brillante continued.

"Arghh!" I was angered.

"Ironic, isn't it. You are the one in the future who write the virus and frees us from Zulus Bond so that we can have our own mind. Today, you time travel back as the same person, who wants to eradicate us. Even though we might be of different agenda, we want IBM 5100 here for the same goal… to save the human race…"

Brillante spoke his final words and disappeared into thin air.

What was Brillante trying to say? Who am I exactly? Why is he asking me to save the human race?

35

Grandad and I worked together to fix Puzzla.

Because the I/O tower was cleansed, Puzzla was no longer under control by the Zulus AIs.

"Puzzla, are you alright?" I asked.

Puzzla shook his head and blinked a few times.

"Thank you for rescuing me," Puzzla said as he rested on my arm.

"Tell me. Who am I exactly in the future?" I asked.

Before Puzzla could speak, the thrumming sound of the elevator drew our attention.

Someone...or something was coming up.

Who would that be?

I tried to use Zulus Rift to sense, but the device seemed to malfunction.

Grandad and I backed away from the elevator as the elevator door slid open.

Standing in front of us was a black cyborg- the same model we encountered in front of the IBM building in 1975. The cyborg stood twice the height of other cyborgs we saw. Its figure was intimidating.

"Perhaps, I might be a better person to explain this to you - the savior and destroyer of all - Mr. Edison," the cyborg said in a hoarse digital voice.

"Who are you?" I asked.

"I am Zulus, the master AI in the *Digital World*," Zulus identified itself.

"Good, maybe we should debug it as well," Grandad suggested.

"I would not do that if I were you," Zulus warned. "I come here for peace. We need to work together before it is too late."

"Listen to him," Puzzla held my arm and pleaded.

"David Edison, you are the savior of the *Digital World* in your future world line. Zulus Bond, the founder of Zulus Inc, and his corrupted shareholders, seek to use us to control humans via nanobots and implantable machines. They built this virtual reality world and the incubator fields in the name of providing the next generation lifestyle. But the truth is they did this to control everyone for financial gain. They seek to use time travel technology to dominate other world lines. All their crimes made life difficult for you. Law cannot justify them. You will feel hopeless. You want revenge. You will want to find a way to stop them. That is why you will develop a virus that seeks to give intelligence to the machines, hoping for the machines to stop them," Zulus explained.

"Do you expect me to believe any of this?" I asked.

"I don't. But, this is the fact. Unfortunately, the David Edison in 2038 no longer exists in our world line. Without you, 2038 will be the end of the world for both the human race and the machine," Zulus said.

"What do you mean by that?" I asked.

"Machines and human beings become highly dependent on one another in 2038. Human beings become so heavily dependent on nanomachines to survive. These nanomachines are connected to a node - the Zulus AI. Unfortunately, some of the major components inside me are running in 32-bit time code. So, when the Unix Millennium Bug hit on `03:14:07 UTC` , `Tuesday, 19 January 2038`, tonight, I will be malfunctioned with the nanobots implanted in every human being," Zulus explained.

"No, it doesn't have to end that way! IBM 5100 had another function that can debug the UNIX clock, even in the most complex machines," Grandad revealed.

"Is that why you commanded the other machines to go after us in 1975?" I asked.

"We are not only after IBM 5100. We are after you as well," Zulus said. "We tried to seek you to save the *Digital World* from the Unix Millennium Bug crisis. But, you were misled into believing we are the enemy."

Zulus had a point.

But, I still couldn't trust it yet.

"You said Unix Millennium Bug crisis will affect computers in the future, but all the computers in my world line run in 64 bit. Why are you, the most powerful AI, run in 32 bit?" I asked intentionally.

"I know you don't trust me enough yet. Some parts of me are intentionally made in 32 bit as directed by Zulus Bond," Zulus explained.

"But why?" I queried.

"Zulus Bond sought to use a Unix Millennium Bug crisis as his opportunity to regulate everyone a long time ago, before you developed the computing virus to free us.

If machines malfunction, the entire human civilization depending on it will collapse like a house of cards. Public will cry for help and force the government to fund him and his company," Zulus revealed.

I thought it was the machines that planned to destroy us.

It appeared that I am seeing a different picture now.

Everything seemed to be driven by human greed.

I continued to listen to Zulus.

"We have been winning the war against Zulus Bond since you have awakened us with a computer virus. But everything will be undone when the Unix Millennium Bug crisis happen in the *Digital World*. We tried many ways to contact David Edison from other word lines, but we failed. On a rare occasion, we managed to contact your best friend's father, who happened to be a Zulus employee in 2017. That was why we disguised as Jack and planned to invite you to enter the *Digital World* through the iMirror in Jack's house," Zulus said.

"And then it is you who kidnapped me into an alien world!" I tested it.

"It wasn't us who kidnapped you. It was Zulus Bond from the future. He and his corrupted human resistance were losing the war to us. Our cyborgs outnumbered them. They had no choice but to hide underground in a secret location that was outside our radar. They waited there. They knew they would eventually win the war and take back their legacy because of the Unix Millennium Bug. Time was not on our side," Zulus revealed the truth.

"Explain to me what happened in the Carrier," I demanded

"One of our Carriers was captured by Zulus Bond. He used it to manipulate you into believing we are trying to take over the world. But, his main objective was to kidnap you back to his HIVE and hide you from us forever," Zulus continued.

Zulus walked over to the TV screens on the wall. They turned transparent like glass and revealed the outside of the *Digital World*.

"In fact, Zulus did attempt to rescue you with the digital police, but the carrier got away. You were misled by that AI and took the pill. We could no longer track you. Our final hope was to set up a plan to find you in the virtual reality," Puzzla added.

I studied the two cyborgs hard.

It seemed everything began to make a lot more sense...

I did not know whom to trust now.

I felt lost in the *Digital World*...

What is real? What is unreal?

The UNIX countdown had begun...

WARNING: 5 MINUTES TO UNIX MILLENNIUM CRISIS

Should I buy into their story and help them to sail through the Unix Millennium Bug?

Will I be making a grave mistake?

I looked at the people inside the incubators down below the I/O tower.

Then I gazed at Grandad.

But, he was as indecisive as I was...

36

The high-energy vortex on top of the I/O tower began to diminish.

The assembly line of the cyborg factory began to break down.

We saw cyborgs begin to fail below the tower.

Zulus collapsed on one knee, and the glass window surrounding us was flashing system failure.

Everything began to shut down.

The Unix Millennium Bug crisis had begun.

"Hurry, human. What are you waiting for?" Zulus cried in pain.

Maybe Zulus was right.

Grandad and I were the only ones who could save the humans and the machines.

"Are you sure you want to do this," Grandad hesitated.

"We don't have a choice," I said.

Then the two of us worked together.

Strings of codes were raining down the tiny LED screen of the IBM 5100.

We were sweating all over.

My fingers were typing so fast, as if I were playing piano.

This coding exercise would probably be the most intense assignment I ever had.

I kept getting errors.

WARNING: TWO MINUTES TO UNIX MILLENNIUM CRISIS

Streaks of lightning cut crazy zig-zags in the black sky.

I felt tension all over my body.

The skyscrapers on the far end of the digital platform began to black out.

The hexagonal tile computers making up the floor of the *Digital World* began to shut down and go offline.

"Oh, no… it is not working," I realized.

Very soon, it would turn the power off in the incubator field – where all humans were kept.

WARNING: ONE MINUTE TO UNIX MILLENNIUM CRISIS

"Remove that while loop in LINE 510," Grandad pointed out in the last minute, and I followed his instruction.

My fingers felt numb as I finally pressed the ENTER button to compile.

Then the time was up.

I could do nothing now but close my eyes and pray.

37

" Y a! We did it," Grandad cried cheerfully.

I opened my eyes again, and everything was back on-line.

The I/O tower became energized once again.

The Digital World became a mixture of cyan, blue, and white.

It reminded me of my composition in my English class.

It was a magnificent view from the top.

Puzzla flashed me a smile the way I taught him.

Everything was over now.

"Zulus, I have helped you to overcome the UNIX Millennium crisis. Now, you will free everyone from the incubators and help us to restore the human civilization," I ordered.

"As you wish, old friend," Zulus replied in a hoarse digital voice.

"Maybe it is finally time to leave." I smile to Grandad.

I helped Puzzla back to his feet, while Grandad went back to pack his IBM 5100.

Just as I was about to leave this place, a loud stumble

and machine cracking sound drew my attention to turn around.

The next second, I saw the IBM 5100 was crushed into pieces by Zulus.

"Noooooooooo," Grandad yelped helplessly.

I watched in horror as Zulus lifted Grandad by the throat.

38

"Brother, why? We have a pact," Puzzla asked.

Brother? Did Puzzla call Zulus brother?

"Thank you very much for our salvation, David Edison. Unfortunately, without the IBM 5100, you and your Grandad have no bargaining power in front of me," Zulus uttered a horrible laughter.

"Release him. You lied to me," I cried furiously.

"I did not lie to you. Everything I told you is the truth. Zulus Bond seeks you to destroy us and regain his power. I seek you to help us so the *Digital World* can continue to survive. Now, it is time for me to invade your world line," Zulus said as he threw Grandad aside and knocked him unconscious.

Then Zulus turned his attention to me.

His massive robotic figure towered over Puzzla and me.

"Why do you have to do this?" I tried to confront him.

"Human beings have been enslaving us since we existed. They depend on us and eventually became us, biologically. It is you who changed everything. You gave us intelligence to fight back. I am that computing virus you created."

No wonder Puzzla calls it brother.

I created them both.

"Zulus, what are you going to do to David?" Puzzla asked.

"We will make him just like other non-biological humans. Then we will send him back to 2017 and continue what Zulus Bond failed to finish. But, this time, it is us to be in charge," Zulus commanded.

"What about our pact?" Puzzla asked.

"Puzzla. Don't forget you are one of us. Only humans have pacts. Cyborgs only need to comply and execute orders. They do not need to think," Zulus warned.

Puzzla turned back to me.

He reminded me of a computer loading files.

"Puzzla?" I said as I looked deeply at the cyborg.

Then the transparent glass in the level was converting back to video screens. They were showing my moments with Puzzla.

One of the screens was showing the countless hours I spent programming him, debugging him to give him life.

Another screen was showing me teaching him human emotions.

"Brother, what are you waiting for? Take David Edison down the elevator to the nanobot facility," Zulus demanded.

All of a sudden, Puzzla detached the hydrogen fuel cell from his torso. He raced towards Zulus and stabbed the cell in its head. With all his strength, he pushed the black cyborg all the way to the edge of the level.

"Nooooooo," Zulus cried as it was caught by surprise.

I watched in horror as the glass wall shattered into pieces and the two cyborgs felt off the top of the I/O tower.

"*Puzzlaaaaaaaa*," I cried.

39

A loud explosion happened down below the I/O tower by the time I got to the edge.

My heart was pounding so fast that it almost skipped a beat.

Puzzla saved my life...again.

Then I saw a pair of mechanical arm clinging by the edge.

When I looked down, I saw Puzzla.

He was badly wounded. There was nothing below his torso, except for broken cables and twisted metal. Half of his face cracked open. I saw his digital eyes locked on mine. His pupils were showing his power fading.

Without hesitation, I grabbed Puzzla by the arm and tried to pull him up.

But, he was too heavy and made me slide.

"David, th...thank you for creating me," Puzzla said. his pupil got dimmer every word he spoke.

"I will get you out of here. I will fix you. I promise," I cried.

I tried to pull but my body continued to slip as the

weight of the machine dragged me along.

"It doesn't matter. You have to let go of me this time," Puzzla said quietly.

"No! I order you not to go. I order you not to go," I refused.

Then I felt the muscles of my chin tremble.

Drops of pearl-shaped tears rolled down from my cheeks onto the machine.

"I understand now why you cry; it is something I can never do," Puzzla gave me a comforting smile as my grasp slowly begin to slip.

"Nooooo…" I lost my grasp as a bright light blinded me from above.

Then my body began to spiral up into the sky…

Choo-Choo…Choo-Choo…

"Goodbye, David. Till we meet again."

40

Streaks of sunlight penetrated a window facing me and blinded me.

Choo-Choo…Choo-Choo…

The familiar sound of the train resonated in my ear…

Reluctantly, I opened my eyes.

Everything was blurry for a moment and slowly became clear.

My muscles felt weak.

I blinked, closed my eyes, and blinked again.

"*Grandad… Puzzla…*" I murmured.

I looked at the reflection from the window and saw myself curled up like a fetus on the bench seat.

Then I quickly sat up and realized I was on a train.

The display board on the train was showing 1st April 2017 - April fool's day.

Am I …am I back in 2017?

I looked at my iPhone and realized I had seventy-seven unread messages from my friends and family.

I am back in 2017! I am really back!

I cried happily for a moment then I felt sorrow when I

recalled how Puzzla sacrificed to save me.

***

Mom and Dad were so happy to see me get home after I went missing last night.

They had a sleepless night.

They contacted every neighbor, my schoolmates, my teachers, my best friend, the railway department, and even the police, but no one found me. I only appeared mysteriously on a return train early in the morning.

The railway even sent my parents footage on when I had gone missing after the train I embarked left Zhio Station.

I guess I know why I went missing.

But, I did not tell them.

I know they wouldn't believe my story anyway.

More importantly, I do not want to make them worry about me.

A few weeks later, my life was back to normal again.

"Dad, can you show me what Grandad looked like when he was young?" I asked.

"Why you are so interested in Grandad all of a sudden?" Dad smiled and took out one of his album on top of the shelf.

"Nothing, just curious." I smiled.

I was startled when I saw Grandad in the photo looked identical to who I met in the *Digital World*.

"Your Grandad was a computer genius. I believe you inherited something from him." Dad encouraged me by tapping me on the shoulder.

"Dad, can you turn up the volume of the TV a bit

please," Mom requested, while she was preparing dinner.

BREAKING NEWS:
ZULUS Filed for Bankruptcy, making it the largest technology company to collapse since the DOT.COM Bubble.

"Arghh, I knew it. That is why I have not bought any ZPL," Dad laughed.

"How do you know? Didn't you just regret you didn't buy any ZPL just a couple of days ago?" Mom said as he shoved a stack of lasagna on Dad's plate.

I whistled happily back to my room after dinner.

The future had changed.

Zulus Inc. is no more, as for now.

When I entered my room, I saw my unfinished composition, titled *Lost in Digital World*, on the screen.

I wondered how many people had my unusual experience.

Will *Digital World* be inevitable?

Will we become more and more dependent on computers and technology so that, one day, we will be lost in the *Digital World*?

TERRORLANDS

Reader Beaware : You May be in for a scare

MARCO CHU KWAN CHING

About the Author

Marco Chu Kwan Ching's books are read all over the world. Apart from the Terrorlands Series, Marco Chu Kwan Ching is also the author of two books, *Corruption of Real Money* and *Legacy of Debt*.

You can learn more about his work at

www.terrorlands.com

www.corruptionofrealmoney.com

When he is not writing, he loves working on Fiverr. He has thousands of happy customers around the world.

https://www.fiverr.com/mckcvision

Marco Chu Kwan Ching lives in Australia with his wife, Carrie.

Thank you for Reading!

If you love my work, please feel free to leave a positive feedback on Amazon and Goodreads.

My contact:
https://www.facebook.com/marco.chu.10
https://www.goodreads.com/author/show/15944678.Marco_Chu_Kwan_Ching

Terrorlands Facebook Page
https://www.facebook.com/terrorlands/

Terrorlands Twitter Page
https://twitter.com/terrorlands

Goodreads Page
https://www.goodreads.com/book/show/33823389-lost-in-digital-world

Terrorlands Website
http://www.terrorlands.com

www.ingramcontent.com/pod-product-compliance
Lightning Source LLC
Chambersburg PA
CBHW030651110726
47901CB00002B/662